Praise for
It's All in the Story

"Every life has its own story, and they are all well-told in _It's All in the Story_. The California you've seen on postcards but never up close is the backdrop for the tales written by talented writers you already know and some you soon will. An intriguing read!"

—**Matt Coyle**, _author of the Anthony Award–winning Rick Cahill crime series_

"SCWA brings together an incredible community of authors, and it shows in this remarkable anthology. By turns gritty, lyrical, sexy, and thrilling, these stories capture the California atmosphere so well you'll be reaching for your sunglasses!"

—**Matthew Quirk**, _New York Times_ bestselling author of The 500 _and_ Dead Man Switch

"D. P. Lyle has built a wonderful anthology, a window on California both wide and focused. Each story is a gem! You don't want to miss this!"

—**Brett Battles**, _USA_ Today _bestselling author of the Jonathan Quinn series_

"You will find it all in *It's All in the Story*. This carefully curated anthology will grab you from the outset and take you on a journey of beautifully rendered stories that are all California through and through. With the conclusion of each short story you will reflect, smile knowingly, and jump into the next one and the one after. The promise is in the title—great stories, expertly told."

—**Ara Grigorian**, *international award-winning author*

"Any good collection of short stories requires emotion, thematic connection, and engaging characters; this book has them all. Dripping with California soul and filled with quirk, pathos, and literary style, *It's All in the Story: California* delivers. If you like short stories, you'll love this collection."

—**Jeff Lyons**, *author of* Anatomy of a Premise Line: How to Master Premise and Story Development for Writing Success

"*It's All in the Story* is a compelling collection of provocative short stories that weave twisting tales across genres and throughout time and space in California. Penned by talented writers, this anthology will intrigue and inspire you to see California and its diverse residents with new eyes."

—**Sheri Fink**, *#1 bestselling children's author, inspirational speaker, and award-winning entrepreneur*

"Whether dark, humorous, or darkly humorous, the tales are infused with the California spirit, often in unexpected ways. A moving, lovingly crafted collection of tales of redemption, loss, and hope."

—**Jacqueline Diamond**, *author of the Safe Harbor Medical Mysteries*

*It's*All
in the
S*t*ory

California

An Anthology of Short Fiction

Edited by D. P. Lyle

Southern California Writers Association
Huntington Beach, CA

SCWA
P.O. Box 47
Huntington Beach, CA 92648
www.ocwriter.com

Publisher's Note: This is a work of fiction. It is a product of the authors' imagination. Any resemblance to people, living or dead, is purely coincidental. Occasionally, real places or institutions are used novelistically for atmosphere. There is no connection between the characters or situations in these stories to any real-life events, people, places, institutions, organizations or companies of any kind.

Ordering Information
Quantity sales. Special discounts are available on quantity purchases by corporations, associations, and others. For details, contact the "Special Sales Department" at the address above.

Orders by US trade bookstores and wholesalers. Please contact BCH: (800) 431-1579 or visit www.bookch.com for details.

Printed in the United States of America

Cataloging-in-Publication data
Names: Lyle, D. P., editor.
Title: It's all in the story : California , an anthology of short fiction / edited by D. P. Lyle.
Description: Huntington Beach, CA: Southern California Writers Association, 2017.
Identifiers: ISBN 978-0-9991243-3-8 (pbk.) | 978-0-9991243-4-5 (ebook) | LCCN 2017951505
Subjects: LCSH Short stories, American--California. | California--Social life and customs--Fiction. | BISA
    FICTION / Anthologies (multiple authors)
Classification: LCC PS3609.T847 I87 2017 | DDC 813.6--dc23

Cover design by Kuo Design.

First Edition

22 21 20 19 18 17   10 9 8 7 6 5 4 3 2 1

Contents

Introduction

Everything begins with an idea.

Whether it's building a skyscraper, walking on the moon, or creating a work of art, the idea comes first. The dream, the vision. Then the hard work of bringing the idea to life begins.

So it was with *It's All in the Story*.

The idea to publish an anthology began in late 2016, when the Southern California Writers Association (SCWA) Board of Directors approved this project, and the work began. When I was asked to serve as editor for this anthology, I was honored and enthusiastically accepted.

The SCWA provides a forum for encouraging and promoting the welfare, fellowship, spirit, and continuing education of published and unpublished writers in the Southern California area. Monthly meetings feature world-class instructors of all genres, experience, and skill levels who share their knowledge and expertise with the members.

And now, an anthology.

Sixty-four stories were submitted for evaluation. The quality of these submissions was exceptional. An editorial committee read and ranked each manuscript, and though each was worthy of inclusion, ultimately, twenty-four were chosen for publication in this edition. During the ranking process, author identities were carefully hidden from the committee, and all rankings were based solely on merit. The result is an amazing collection of stories.

Everything begins with an idea.

This is particularly true in storytelling. It's the classic What If? What if this happened? Or maybe that? What would happen next? How would this, or that, affect the protagonist? What responses would it invoke? What feelings and emotions would it stir? What pressures, complications, and obstacles would test the hero? This is the stuff of great fiction.

This is how every story begins—and develops.

Many believe that writing a short story is easier than writing a novel. I mean, doesn't creating 3,000, 5,000, or 10,000 words require less effort than hammering out 100,000? In many respects, this is true. A novel takes more time, there are more elements to weave together, and characters and plots must be developed more deeply. But with longer fiction, the writer has more "room." Room to thoroughly explore characters, to devise more complex plots, to offer brighter descriptions, to write longer dialogue exchanges, and to craft more exposition that deepens and cements the story.

In shorter fiction, there is much less room to maneuver. Each of the above elements must also be addressed, but the reduced word count puts significant limitations on the author. Developing empathetic characters, interesting plot twists, sparkling dialogue, and vivid settings is no less important, but in shorter fiction, the telling must be economical, concise, and chiseled. No easy task.

Each of the authors who submitted stories for this anthology faced this challenge head-on, and all acquitted themselves well.

Each included story roots itself in California—-the history, geography, culture, and the wonderfully quirky folks who inhabit the "Left Coast." The stories span from 1812 San Juan Capistrano to the California gold rush to the modern-day Newport Coast.

In this collection, you will find heroism, tragedy, humor, and both realized and broken dreams. You will "hear" many voices and meet a host of memorable characters, each facing unique personal challenges.

A young woman, struggling with her past, unsure of her future, and looking for that interpersonal connection that will allow her to smile again. A couple, both damaged—she by abandonment and a fractured heart; he by war, a broken body, and undeserved guilt. Can love survive that? A would-be photographer who shoots aging surf musicians and a famous-for-being-famous star, both making their own "California Promise."

We will meet three Cal Tech nerds as they plan to break Vegas; a concert pianist who is damaged both physically and emotionally; a pair of bank robbers who get much more than they bargained for; siblings who take their high desert "full service" gas station to an entirely new level; and even William Randolph Hearst, the vampire.

You will encounter star-crossed lovers divided by culture, race, and social standing; a fallen angel on a quest and on the run; a demon who devours souls; and a "Kick the Bucket" tour operator as she ferries tourists past famous LA murder sites. You will meet a young boy who seeks the impossible pot of gold at the end of the rainbow only to cross paths with a robber of long-forgotten Southern California graves and a killer who must dispose of a body in a Disneyland motel. Who's the real victim here?

And so many more wonderful characters and fascinating tales.

So, I invite you inside. Get comfy, sit a spell, and enjoy these re-markable stories. Each is beautifully written and thought provoking and will linger with you long after the last page.

Welcome to *It's All in the Story*.

After the Wave Breaks

Jo Ellen Pitzer

Grams isn't supposed to be here. This floor is nothing like the rehab wing of the hospital. Pale-peach walls, white tile floors, and that pervasive sterile stench.

I approach the nurses' station. An older woman wrapped in a light sweater talks on the phone. She holds up a finger: *Just a sec.* Farther down, a crowd is gathered outside a patient's room. There's gotta be ten people there at least. A bad feeling pulls me over.

The number outside the room matches Grams's. My heart drops to my gut. I go on tippy-toes to see, but my view's blocked. The nurse standing next to me has a thin mustache that creeps me out a little. He's joking with a patient attached to an IV pole. I'm almost relieved. Surely they wouldn't stand here laughing if Grams were in trouble.

"She can't stand on the scale," he's saying. "So they had to use that."

The crowd moves back to make room for what Nurse Mustache is referring to. It's a seven-foot-tall contraption with a hook at the top. It reminds me of that arcade game where you maneuver the claw to grab the prize. Two women in matching yellow scrubs roll it through the door and down the hall.

"It picks up everything. Bed and all," Mustache goes on. "We know the bed's weight. Subtract it, and we get hers."

"So they weighed her like cattle?" *Ahh-hahahaha.* The patient winces. Braces his stomach. "Like a beached whale? No. Wait. A lame—"

I shove past them. Inside, yet another nurse is tucking sheets around Grams.

"I can't weigh that much. Next time we do it without the bedding."

Her voice is hoarse. Skin pale. I go straight to her bed. Grab the rails. "Grams!" She turns, and my heart remembers to beat again. The spark's still in her eyes. "You're okay?"

"Katelyn, honey. It's good to see you."

"What's going on?"

"We had some trouble settling in," the nurse says in a tone you'd use for a kindergartener, not a sixteen-year-old. "But we're good now. You missed the fun."

I snap my head in her direction. "I didn't miss the way everyone's laughing at her."

"Of course they're laughing," Grams cuts in. "It's *funny.*" "Humiliating" is the word I would've picked. I should know. But Grams goes on, oblivious. "Besides, smiles are my brand of medicine. A good one heals you, body and soul. I'll bet there isn't a sniffle around here for days."

I swear Grams's life mission is to get others to smile. You'd think it'd cure cancer the way she talks. I play along and try it. The corners of my lips falter. I don't like the idea of her being the joke of the day. She grins back, but there's something in her eyes. Sadness? Pity? My smile doesn't do any good.

"Did you get to the beach today?" she says. "I need my ions."

Negative ions, she means. It's another crazy-Grams thing. Supposedly, a cloud of them gets released when waves crash on the shore. They've got healing properties. Not as much as smiles, but still.

"As promised." I reach my hands out to her. "Go ahead and take them."

"I'm not sure it works that way." She chuckles, but rubs my hands anyway.

In the morning, I head to Huntington Beach for my daily ion gathering. Grams walks this shore every day and expects to do so until the day she dies. It was why she agreed to the double knee replacement. Wheelchairs don't cut it on the sand. The surgery went as expected. With lots of therapy, her knees'll be fine. What wasn't expected was the spray of blood clots in her lungs, which jacked up her heart two days later.

I spread my arms out. Determined to collect as many stupid ions as I can.

This place is nothing like Oregon. A few steps from Mom's back door and you're lost in the trees. It's where I met my best friend, Cassie. Follow the trail to the stream and it's where I had my first kiss. Over by the rocks is where Jax waited for me. It's also the place I found him and Cassie a month later.

This beach is nothing like I remember as a kid, either. Summer vacations in Southern California meant hot sand, burning skies, bathing suits, and boogie boards. Surf City was a kaleidoscope of color, teeming with people.

It's different now. For starters, this early-morning, late-winter beach is empty. It's like a painting done up in muted grays. A thick layer of mist hangs low over the dark water. The sand is bleached almost silver in this light. A few surfers dot the waves. On the pier, fishermen stand guard over their poles. And the occasional pass-ersby seem more like scenery than real people.

On the water, a tall wave rises. It takes my breath away. It's pow-erful. Strong. *Alive.* I want it to stay like this forever. Instead, it crashes spectacularly, the force of it no doubt releasing Grams's ions into the air. Turbulent white water barrels toward me, but soon the wave's roar dwindles into a soft sizzle. My shoulders sag. In a matter of seconds, that magnificent wall of strength has been reduced to a few inches of empty water, stripped of whatever had held it together. A few remaining bubbles pop and crackle as the water's vulnerable edge reaches the tips of my shoes. I bend down, reach out, and try to hold it here. Where it's safe. But the ocean drags it back, and what's left of the wave slips through my fingers.

As I straighten up, three surfers wade back to shore. One catches my eye. The taller one, with the dark hair. He goes to my school. I glance away. Try to convince myself he's just background. Part of the scenery. That nothing's changed. But the flutter in my chest won't let me.

The flutter's still lingering when I'm in Mrs. Kinoshita's flower shop after school. Mrs. K lives in the apartment next to Grams. She hired me two months ago, right after I moved in. I think she felt sorry for me.

"This is for your grandmother." She's holding a bouquet of flowers in a golden-green vase that matches her eyes. She's a hiker, and her skin has the look of someone who's spent a lot of time outdoors. It makes her seem old and young at the same time.

"These are gorgeous." I take the flowers from her. "She's gonna love them."

"It's nothing." She waves me off, but I can tell she's proud of her creation. She should be. It really is beautiful. As she starts to gather her things, she asks, "You coming tonight? I discovered the caramel-filled churros last week. Ah-mazing."

She's talking about Surf City Nights, the weekly farmers' market and street fair. Mrs. K and her friend run a stall there. I've never been, but Grams has. There's fresh food and live music. I'm tempted to go. This surprises me. It scares me a little, too.

"Not tonight," I say.

My promise to Grams keeps me strolling the beach every morning. I go earlier so I'm less likely to run into Nick Romero coming in to shore. (Yes, I found out his name.) He's out there now. A glorious wave rises up behind him. I stop and hold my breath, willing it to last. But it falters, like always. I'm about to walk away when I see Nick jump onto his board. And this time, despite the wave crumbling, I'm not disappointed. Because whatever forces tear it down also propel Nick forward. He's filled with an exhilaration that's obvious as he slices his board through the water. He lets out a *whoop*, and I almost echo it. He cuts a sharp turn, and before I know it, he's flat on his stomach. Paddling hard. Hungry for more. Behind him, the water's edge surges toward me, slows, and recedes.

This time I don't try to stop it.

Back in Grams's room, there's a strange machinelike thing on the floor.

"That torture device?" Grams says when I ask about it. "They dropped it off this morning."

"It's for her knees, but we can't figure it out." This from a new nurse. Her blond ponytail bobs back and forth as she looks up from the clipboard in her hand and over to me. She shrugs, as if it's funny. Then she focuses back on the machines crowding Grams's bed.

"What do you mean?"

"We don't do much PT on the telemetry floor. I don't know what to do with that."

"How 'bout strap in her legs and turn it on?"

"Honey, this is Brianne," Grams interrupts. She's reminding me of my manners. "She's been so helpful to me. Brianne, my granddaughter Katelyn."

I force a tight smile, as if knowing Brianne's name makes a difference to Grams's knees.

That night my sister calls. Lane's exactly thirteen months older than me, and I miss her like crazy. She's beyond thrilled. Her team didn't just sweep the tournament; they killed it. And the college recruiters witnessed it all. There were two messages from coaches waiting for her by the time she got home. I'm not surprised. My sister's a rock star on the pitcher's mound.

"You have to send me pictures," I say. "Grams will wanna see them, too." She'll have posted a ton, but we both know the Internet's an ugly place for me.

There's silence on the line, and my stomach knots up. "You know," she starts slowly, as if reading my thoughts. "It's not so bad now." She's treading carefully. This is a topic we don't discuss much. "There's nothing new. Most of the old stuff's been taken down, too. It's almost like it didn't happen." I suck in a breath. She notices. "I mean, I know it happened, but . . . you know."

I don't know how to respond to this. Lane breaks the awkwardness by asking about Grams. I blow out a breath, relieved that we've moved on to her latest debacle.

"All she wants is to walk the beach. If she doesn't start rehab soon, who knows if she'll be able to."

"It'll be fine, Kate. Everything works out the way it's supposed to."

"Whatever." I shake my head. "You and Grams. You're both so glass half full. I've yet to hear her complain. If she wasn't in the hospital, you'd never know she was sick. It's as if she thinks it's her job to keep everyone else happy."

"That's Grams for ya. Smiles are her—"

"I know. I know. Her brand of medicine. God, you sound just like her." I pause. "I wish you were here."

There's a familiarity to the hospital now. I don't like that. They've moved Grams farther away from the nurses' station. It's a smaller room. Fewer machines. I poke my head in, careful not to disturb her if she's sleeping.

Grams is on her back with her graying hair splayed over the pillow. Auntie Ada stands at her bedside combing through it with long, smooth strokes. I think about the hours Lane and I spent playing with each other's hair. There's something special about those times. I don't want to ruin this moment for these sisters.

Grams is talking with her eyes closed. Auntie's hard of hearing, so Grams speaks up. "They say my rhythm's controlled, and I'm not so short of breath now."

"Good. You'll be going home soon, then?"

"Yep. Me and the torture sticks."

Auntie puts the comb down, gathers all Grams's hair in her hands, and twists it around her fingers. "It's that bad, huh?"

"I've got pills for the pain," she says. "But they make me so damn tired."

"I know." It's as if Auntie's communicating a million things with those two little words. She starts to comb Grams's hair again. "I'm sorry."

They still haven't noticed me, and I'm not sure what to do. Stay? Go? I don't want to interrupt. Grams needs someone to listen in a way only a sister can.

Before I decide, I hear Auntie *tsk*. "They call this shampoo? This stuff's pathetic." She picks the can of dry shampoo off the tray table. I said the same thing when I brought it in the other day. She squints at the label, then sets the can down between a box of tissues and the book Grams begs me to read to her. The cover must catch her eye because she grabs it and says, "You read this smut?"

"What?" Grams opens her eyes reluctantly. "Oh, that. I make Katelyn read it to me." She runs her fingers through her hair. Auntie gets the hint and starts combing again. Grams closes her eyes and sighs. "You should see the way she blushes when she gets to the racy parts. It's a hoot. Does my heart good."

I back up into the hall, embarrassed that I've been eavesdropping, mortified that Grams is conning me. I sink to the ground as it all comes swarming back. Jax and Cassie. The snickers that followed. The online explosion—post after post—that tore my life apart. I thought I left it all behind when I came to California.

I feel two inches tall and sick to my stomach when Grams's words replay in my head. *It does my heart good.*

"I got one more last night," she says. I lean back on the wall and strain to hear, though I know I shouldn't. "Her name's Lucy. She comes every night to clean the room and empty the trash. Sweet thing, barely says a word. But I did it. I *finally* got my smile."

It does my heart good.

Suddenly I understand. All those people smiling and laughing around Grams. It does *her* good. It's what *she* needs.

"Well done," my great-aunt says. I hear the smile in her voice, too. "I know that took effort."

"It was worth it." Then, after a pause, "I just need one more."
I know who she's talking about. Me. She needs *my* smile.

The next morning I go find it. It's been so long since I've smiled
for real, I worry that I've forgotten how. Grams will know the difference. She says a true smile is contagious. I try the pier first. Smile
hello to the fishermen. See if they catch mine and return it. The ones
not struggling with their lines nod back over steaming cups of coffee,
but that's it. No smiles. Maybe they don't think I'm sincere. Maybe
they're right. I feel foolish but keep trying. I see a toddler in a stroller.
I bend over and wave. Her eyes go wide, and I think I might've done
it. Until she throws her doll at me and starts to wail. I pick it up and
hand it to her haggard-looking mother, along with a smile. She glares
in return, exasperated.

On the beach, it's worse. Joggers huff and puff their way past with
barely a glance. An elderly couple with metal detectors never even
look up.

This is stupid, I say to myself. This plan seemed perfect when I left
the hospital yesterday. But seriously. What am I thinking? It makes
as much sense as Grams's negative ions. Which reminds me. I face
the water, inhale, and suck some down.

Nick and his friends are out there, of course. They line up for the
next set of waves. He rides a beautiful one all the way in. He seems so
relaxed. At peace. As if his troubles are nonexistent.

I'm seeing the ocean in a whole new way. I'm not focused on
the crashing down part but on what comes after. Negative ions for
Grams. A perfect ride for Nick. I watch as the last bit of wave creeps
toward my toes, pauses, and then pulls back. This time I know it's not
trying to escape the ocean. It's going back for more. To see what else
it can do. And it's begging me to join it.

The weird thing is, I want to.

Then it hits me. *This* is why Grams wants me here. For this feeling I'm having right now.

I expect Nick to paddle back out, but he doesn't. He heads toward shore, riding high from that last wave. God, he has the best smile. It's like he can't help it.

I want that, too.

This time, when he catches my eye, I don't look away. My lips turn up at the corners. It's small, but it's a start.

"Hey," I say when he's close enough to hear. Butterflies scatter in my stomach. "Take me out there sometime?" We're both surprised by my request.

He recovers first. "You bet." His friends are calling, but he's reluctant to go. "Um. See ya at school?"

I nod, shocked that Nick recognizes me. He nods back, and that's enough for now. He catches up with his friends.

I spin toward the water and remember to breathe.

Two days later Grams is released. Instead of driving home, she makes me take her to the beach. We sit in the car. Stare out the windshield. The ocean looks different this time of day. As the afternoon sun drops toward the horizon, it leaves a golden trail across the water that continues all the way out to where it meets the sky. We roll down the windows and breathe in the salty air.

And the ions.

We say nothing for a long time. Eventually Grams takes ahold of my hand. "Are you ready to go home?"

A wave crashes, sending a spray of water in the air. Sunlight bounces off of it in tiny rainbows. It steals my breath, and I feel a smile forming from the inside out. I turn to show Grams.

"I'm already there."

Angel of the Morning

D. J. Phinney

Fullerton, California: September 18, 1968

It's him, as sure as Hades, in her section of the Denny's: Victor Malone, the boy she'd slept with in September 1950. Ginny'd met him at the Pike, in uniform, in line behind her, clutching a quarter in his fist to take four snapshots in a photo booth. He'd been an army private with orders to Fort Ord and then Korea. It had been his eighteenth birthday. His driver's license had proved it.

He'd been alone. He'd said, "Virginia, I might not be comin' home." They'd shared a five-day whirlwind tour, exploring Southern California: Knott's, the Great White Steamer, Hollywood, and Griffith Park. Their last night beneath the stars at Tin Can Beach, they'd both surrendered their virginity and kept each other warm.

At dawn she'd watched him sleep. Struggled not to fall in love. Sunrise over Bolsa Bay greeted the sandpipers.

He'd awakened, fired up his Ford, driven to Long Beach.

At the Red Car station, he hadn't even kissed or touched her cheek. He'd just said, "Thank you, ma'am," and let her walk away.

Disappointed, Ginny had wondered what she'd done to make him mad.

Two days later, he'd shipped out to Korea.

Ginny hadn't gotten mad for years.

But on his birthday, here he is, eighteen years later, exactly to the day. His scar-pitted muscled arms are typical of car mechanics. A pack of Camels fills a pocket of his ironed sun-bleached shirt with its Union 76 orange-and-blue Minute Man emblem. Above the right pocket, his name, in blue embroidered letters, VIC.

What? He thinks I have a duty?

Well, she doesn't. She ignores him, stuffs her order pad and pen into her apron. At 5:00 a.m. he eats his "country-fresh fried eggs," sips his "Denny's Special Coffee" in her window booth. He's not getting a freebie.

Any freebie. Not even his Denny's birthday breakfast.

He broke her heart. She dreads even a peek into those eyes. Once, she'd thought she had found love there. Her innocence had cost her heart.

His innocence had gone to war.

Still, he'd written, "Miss you, Ginny."

Thrilled, she'd written back, mailed those snapshots of herself from the Pike, wearing her pink pullover sweater he'd said flattered her.

Every night in Buena Park, she'd checked her mailbox.

No letters.

After a year, she'd given up. Married Leonard for eighteen months, until the bastard beat her up a second time.

Now she keeps men at arm's length. She's convinced they only break things. Victor broke her heart, and her ex-husband broke her jaw. Best to preserve your heart in cold storage. Stuff emotions. Play it safe.

She'd never known if Vic was dead or if he'd found another woman. She'd called the Pentagon. Of thirty-seven thousand damn obituaries, Victor Malone's name wasn't among them.

Now he shows up wanting "coffee." *Screw him.* He's staring at a photograph. He hides it every time Ginny walks by. He glances at her. Ginny's hoping Victor won't remember. Maybe he's just a stranger who resembles him.

A lot.

Save for a mess of ugly scars on his left cheek and a keloid where it seems Korea shredded off the bottom of one ear, scars as pink as Double Bubble.

One glance makes Ginny wince.

Victor brings his coffee to his lips.

He meets her gaze.

That photo strip he hides beneath his palm.

Snapshots from the Pike she'd mailed him in 1950!

"Virginia?" His voice is gravelly.

Shivers travel up her spine.

She goes by Maggie, not Virginia, now. In high school she'd been "Ginny." She's too slutty for Virginia. Magdalena seems more honest.

He sets his cup down on a napkin.

"Someone tell you I was here?" she asks.

"Coincidence."

"Liar. It's been eighteen years. Exactly."

"You remember." He looks away.

"Yup," she says. "You never wrote."

Virginia pours his coffee until it overtops his cup.

"I wrote two letters."

"Funny, I only got *one*."

"Well, there were two." He's staring at her hand. "Perhaps I wrote but Uncle Sam's Misguided Children never delivered my second letter."

Her ring finger feels naked. His eyes look cloudy, as if he's learned to cover pain beneath a thick haze of indifference.

Same way she has. She hides it better, if anybody cares.

Life has messed her up, same way it messed up Victor's face. She'd been gorgeous when she'd climbed out of his slate-gray Ford Deluxe. It was the last time Ginny'd cried.

He looks away from Ginny's memories. Typical.

She just wishes she knew how to release them.

North of Hagaru-ri, North Korea: 27 November 1950, 1800 Hours

Victor heard it on the radio from Tokyo. MacArthur's predicting they'll spend Christmas in Japan. The news cheers Regimental Combat Team RCT 31. They've battled since September. Hell might freeze, but the soldiers smile, hoping war's atrocity might end.

The axle underneath him jars his spine as they traverse frozen land-scapes on roadways notched like shelves through treeless cliffs. Outside, winds howl. Riding a troop carrier with rust holes through the truck bed, Vic listens to weary fellow soldiers. It's thirty-five below out, so cold the powdered snow mixes with dust in pale clouds, revealing their position.

Victor frowns and stomps his feet to warm his toes.

He crams a fist into an armpit, blows air to thaw his other fingers. Exhales ice crystals.

"Cold enough?" somebody asks.

He grunts. Stares out the back. The geniuses at headquarters don't under-stand Korean winters. They've equipped troops with summer gear for their "mop-up operation." Men wear everything they have: woolen undies, extra socks, pile jackets beneath wind-resistant parkas. Scarves are lashed around their heads, doubled up over their ears beneath their helmets. Victor has no feeling in one ear.

At Hagaru-ri they left eight men at the marine base, frostbite casualties. South Korean FNGs, Fucking New Guys, took their places. Vic doubts they'll survive unless this war wraps up by Christmas.

The motorcade stops. Army engineers repair the road. Freezing troops assemble outside, exercising to stay warm. The winter sears Vic's lungs and makes his muscles burn.

He smells campfires. They will spend the night here.

For years Ginny's been angry. After topping off Victor's coffee, she storms off. There's a wall Ginny's crafted out of ice she can't break through.

She stops.

Why did Victor keep my picture?

Clearly Vic hasn't forgotten.

But he lied.

Ginny steels herself to find out why.

28 November, 0100 Hours

Their light machine guns don't work in the cold. This is especially true at night when it hits forty below zero. You need to jack them back by hand, firing one round at a time, unless you get one of the heavy guns and fill their water jackets with antifreeze. There aren't enough good guns to go around.

Victor lights himself a Camel. No warm-up tents tonight. Chicoms have been sighted. Reinforcements have lost contact. Marines told Colonel Faith there might be three Chinese divisions in this sector.

Men dig into position.

After they chop through ten inches of icy dirt, the digging gets easy, few stones and fewer trees with any roots. The land is barren.

Colonel Faith sets a command post just behind their new perimeter.

After midnight, everything is quiet.

The first enemy probe occurs at 0100 hours. The Chinese fire, and men shoot back when they're told not to.

That tells the Communists their army has encountered UN forces.

Chicoms melt away into the night.

Soon thousands of Chinese on the ridgelines rain down mortar fire. They circle the right flank, firing American-made Tommy guns, seizing a mortar. Gaps form in the lines on the perimeter. Colonel MacLean calls for retreat. Vic trips over Chinese corpses and continues firing one shot at a time.

A grenade explodes.

The FNG in front of him collapses. Blood squirts out behind his knee. Moans attract enemy fire. Vic can't reach him.

There must be thousands of Chinese lighting hillsides with their gunfire. That noisy FNG has died.

Daybreak reveals carrier-based Corsairs, counterattacking.

Antiaircraft guns shoot skyward.

For now the Chinese can't advance. Men shoot grenades to show the Corsairs where to bomb. It isn't helping.

Vic sprints into the encampment. Someone screams into the radio, "We have ourselves a Charlie-Foxtrot," Army speak for cluster-fuck.

Victor bites his lip. He swallows terror.

Virginia clears her throat. "You want a warm-up on that coffee?"

He looks away.

"Been a long time, Vic," she says.

She digs her fist into her hip. She isn't sure whether to slap Victor or ask about the snapshots. A corner of the photo strip has fractured off like glass.

Ginny sucks her cheeks in. *Those photographs. I look so innocent!*

Victor glances at her. Grins.

Ginny sees him swallow.

Hard.

Maybe Vic still has a soul, despite how badly he has wounded her.

She wonders if she has a soul herself.

While medics bandage up the wounded, one hundred casualties lie on cots outside the aid station, and body bags are stacked like cords of wood.

A chopper thunders toward a rice paddy.

BOHICA, Vic thinks. Bend over, here it comes again.

Lieutenant General Ned Almond, commander of the X Corps, is paying one of his legendary visits. He strides toward the camp to have a chat with Colonel Faith.

Everybody stays out of his way.

A bugle call. The general would like a little ceremony.

All snap to attention.

General Almond retrieves three Silver Stars from his pocket. He gives the first to Colonel Faith, selects two soldiers at random, pins medals to their parkas, then addresses all the men. "The enemy delaying you is nothing more than remnants of Chinese divisions fleeing north. We're still attacking, and we're going all the way north to the Yalu. Don't let a bunch of Chinese laundrymen distract you."

Almond climbs aboard his helicopter and rises toward safety.

"Bullshit," Colonel Faith mouths, tearing off his Silver Star. He throws it down into the snow, whirls to face his men. "Better get your positions in good tonight," he mutters, "or there won't be any positions tomorrow morning."

"Yup, that's you," Victor murmurs. "Didn't mean no harm . . ."

"What did your *second* letter say?"

"The one I sent from the marine base? Don't remember."

"Yes, you do." She plops her coffeepot on the table and sits down. "I wrote I loved you in my letter. What did *you* write? After eighteen years, I *need* to know the truth."

He looks down at her photos, not at her.

29 November, 0600 Hours

Chinese burp guns are butt ugly, but they spread typhoons of lead. Their noise is the most frightening sound Victor's ever heard. Brrrrrap-pap-pap-pap-pap-pap. Their racket echoes off the mountains. PPSh-41 submachine guns rain bullets into the encampment.

The men, now dug in deeper than a tick in a hound's hide, receive orders to retreat while still engaging Chinese fire. One hundred twenty-seven wounded are loaded onto truck beds, leaving no room for equipment. They will leave it all behind: kitchen provisions, ammunition, medical supplies. If they burn it, fires will reveal their position. Chinese roam the barren mountainsides like colonies of ants.

Victor has a nasty feeling in his gut.

Soon Chinese attack in successive human waves. Colonel Faith thinks he's outnumbered, eight to one.

RCT 31 fights hand to hand, using bayonets and tools. No time to bury the dead or help the wounded. Vic glances up to see three parachutes from Corsairs drop supplies, badly needed food and ammunition. But winds blow their supplies to Chinese outside the perimeter. Victor's heart sinks.

He spots two Chicom infiltrators. Kills them.

Across a finger of ice along the edge of the Chosin Reservoir, gunfire echoes from positions everyone assumed were friendly. Colonel MacLean hollers to stop, walking out onto the ice.

He's hit.

He staggers, collapsing near the other side, disappearing into fog.

Shit, that wasn't friendly fire!

Colonel Faith counterattacks. The ice is littered with Chinese. Sixty-eight kills are confirmed. The road's been cleared.

But there's no trace of MacLean. They're surrounded in a field, having ridgelines on three sides loaded with Chicoms. Fields of ice span the Chosin Reservoir, their sole path of retreat.

And that reservoir ice won't support their motorcade.

1 December, 0900 Hours

They have been holed up in the same position for seventy-two hours. More than one thousand are dead. Most surviving men are wounded. Due to unexpected weather, air support's been discontinued.

Reinforcements still haven't arrived.

There's no more surgical equipment, no morphine, no bandages. Medics improvise with undershirts and towels. At 1100 hours, a marine Corsair appears, radioing no reinforcements are en route.

Colonel Faith informs his troops, "We'll need to break through the perimeter. Dash to safety. Can't afford to risk another night here. Select your twenty-two best vehicles. Leave the rest behind. We're low on fuel. The dead will ride. Everyone else walks."

They destroy their other vehicles with phosphorus grenades and form a column heading south. Victor walks beside a truck. On point, Company C mans a dual forty-millimeter half-track.

Enemy bullets whistle past.

Friendly planes in close support miss their target, dropping napalm onto the half-track. It explodes. Men roll through snow, beating the flames out.

Colonel Faith rounds up survivors. A Chinese roadblock stops the trucks. Grenade fragments shred through Victor's cheek. His blood is freezing. He fights on, joining eighty-some-odd men and Colonel Faith to clear the road-block. But Faith is badly wounded.

They load the dying colonel into a truck cab.

The cold sun disappears.

They walk out onto the ice.

Victor staggers on by moonlight, needing something to believe in. Virginia's snapshots are in his wallet, but if he removes his gloves he'll lose his fingers.

Besides, he cannot see her in the dark.

2 December, 0400 Hours

After an ambush of the fifteen trucks remaining, with no officers, no food or ammunition. winds have cleared snow from the ice. Victor races against time.

He needs to find Hagaru-ri.

It's on the shoreline. If he walks fast enough, he'll find it.

Brrrrrap-pap-pap-pap-pap-pap. Bullets ricochet off ice.

He has no feeling in his legs. He's touched his face. Something is wrong. He staggers toward a wounded soldier, throws the man across his shoulders. Tries to lift him, glad for warmth.

The sergeant coughs up blood.

"Don't die on me, you bastard," Victor whispers.

No pulse. No breathing.

"Dammit!" Victor says. The warmth from the dead mass has thawed his fingers just enough. Victor fumbles for his wallet.

And that snapshot of Virginia.

Finding strength to stumble on.

Warmth he remembers.

He trudges south.

For hours.

At 0945, he staggers into Hagaru-ri.

The marines tell him his unit faces court-martial for desertion.

Marine General O. P. Smith hopes they'll spend some time at Leavenworth.

"A few laundrymen," he says, "and you assholes cut and run."

They have it wrong, but no marine backs army grunts against a two-star marine general who dismisses the survivors. The damn marines listened to Almond, who bullshitted MacArthur, got his troops overextended. Almond won't admit his error.

Stunned, Victor has no recourse. He's grieving friends, exhausted.

All his officers are dead. Not one soldier brought them home.

For three more years in other units, Victor knows he'll fight his best.

But henceforth he'll be branded a deserter.

Fullerton:
1968

Her shift's over. He's been staring at her snapshots thirty minutes. Ginny touches Victor's fingers. They are colder than a milk shake.

She hopes to figure out what she did wrong. "You okay?"

He shoves the photo strip in her direction.

She asks again, "What did you write? I checked my mailbox for months. Did you ever write me back?"

"Ginny, I lied." He takes a breath. "Never mailed my second letter." He shivers, choking up. Evidently, one of Victor's tears has melted.

"Dammit. I loved you." She wants to slap him, but he's finally told the truth.

"I was ashamed."

"Ashamed of *what*?"

His head ratchets in her direction as if he wills himself to face her. "I loved your memory." He seems to peer into her soul like she remembers in the backseat of his Ford. "A navy chaplain with the marines asserts we threw down all our weapons, cut and ran, abandoned two commanding officers to Chicoms. General Smith labeled us cowards. I don't deserve you, Ginny Thomas."

"Who in bloody hell is General Smith?"

"With the marines."

She leans forward. "Victor, please tell me what happened."

"Don't want to. Dammit, Ginny, I don't want to."

She cups Vic's frozen hands inside her fists and meets his gaze, fearing he can see clear to Korea. Survivor's guilt, combat fatigue. So many names civilians use for conditions they refuse to understand.

But as a woman who's been battered, Ginny has a hint. If she reaches him, she rescues herself, too. "Tell me, Vic," she whispers. "You didn't come here to drink coffee. No one can reach us if we lock our doors and board up all our windows."

He wraps his hands around her coffeepot and stares toward the doors. His gaze returns to hers. "Buddies were scattered on the ice. Bodies stretched past the horizon, limbs black with frostbite." Tears wet Victor's cheeks, and he grates out, "The damn Chinese took all our shoes."

He's weeping now. She listens to the horror and the shame for forty minutes.

His hands are warm enough to finally touch her cheek.

She caresses his cheek, too. His keloid feels like a heart. His smile breaks, and she is back at Tin Can Beach, watching sandpipers and wishing she had somebody to share it with.

"It's your birthday," Ginny whispers. "I'll buy breakfast."

"Isn't it . . . free?"

"Perhaps we both are now, Vic. Ever been to Nu-Pike?"

Victor's head shakes.

"My shift ended at seven. Can you drive?"

He takes her hand, escorts her to the front seat of his Ford.

It's being restored. Restoration is a miracle, she thinks.

Victor cranks the V8 engine and drapes an arm across her shoulder.

She snuggles close.

He turns right onto Harbor, cruising south.

Ginny grins. It feels damn fine being warm.

House at Pooh Corner

Julie Wells

Everybody knows that it's not the snow that will kill you. It's what happens when the temperature falls below thirty-two degrees and, instead of snow, an icy drizzle begins to fall. The liquid freezes upon impact, glazing the asphalt with transparent sheets of deadly destruction. In South Lake Tahoe, we call it black ice: the invisible killer. Right up there with cancer, carbon monoxide, and of course, Flint, Michigan, drinking water.

This story takes place in a time before cell phones. Is that hard for you to even imagine? Now I know something about you! Leaving work that fateful winter night, I battled my way through crosstown traffic. I lived in California but worked at a casino in Nevada just a few miles away. Dealing blackjack was not the most exciting job, but it paid the bills. The worst of the snow was now behind us. The roads were mostly thawed, showing dollops of dirt-colored snow heaped here and there. Some jerk in a hurry spun out at Ski Run Boulevard, hit a UPS truck head-on, and held up traffic for the better part of an hour. Tourists!

Thankfully, I slid into the day care parking lot two minutes before overtime fees kicked in, only to discover that another form of punishment awaited me. The frizzy-haired, redheaded "teacher" (and I use that word loosely) could not understand why my one-year-old, Brady, refused to take a nap. How would I know? Wasn't she the so-called expert on children? After being held captive another grueling five minutes and pretending to really give a _____ (feel free to fill in the blank), I was finally released.

Brady and his three-year-old brother, Taylor, were exhausted, and thankfully did not fight me as I buckled them into their car seats. Work was over, but now my real job began.

Pulling out of the day care driveway onto the main road, I pondered which way to go. The safest, surest route home was simply staying on Highway 50 to Emerald Bay, but a fuzzy thought was slowly forming in my brain. My friend Suzanna had called me that morning saying that she'd had car trouble. She had ended up walking to work. It had been really cold lately, with temperatures below zero. Showers of light drizzle had been falling throughout the day. I could not imagine the poor thing trudging through the dusk in the bitter chill. I looked at the clock; the timing was perfect! If I turned left at Black Bart, I could pick her up right as she was leaving the elderly woman's home where she was a caretaker. But should I?

Knowing that my tired, hungry kids would have preferred the direct route home, I weighed my options. Which would be better? Take good care of my kids or take good care of my friend? How many times a day do we do that? See a fork in our mind, with two outstretched roads? Now that I've learned more about quantum mechanics, I guess it's more accurate to say there were an infinite number of roads I could have taken that night. I made a decision, turned off Highway 50 and onto Black Bart. I wryly thought to myself, I chose the "road less traveled." How poetic. Little did I know then that this seemingly small decision would result in a significant celestial outcome.

As I turned off the main road, we entered a sparsely populated wooded area. I had been to the home of the old lady (oops, I mean youthfully challenged female) only once before, and I was hoping I could find it again in the dark. Climbing the hill, I felt the tires losing traction as we hit patches of ice, so I slowed down. The kids began poking at each other; it was only a matter of time before someone would be screaming. I switched the CD player to their favorite song, "House at Pooh Corner" by Kenny Loggins.

"Wheeeeeeeee!" both boys exclaimed as we hit a large patch of ice and our minivan spun in a complete circle, sliding toward the yellow dividing line. Don't panic, I told myself. I slowly turned the wheel the opposite direction of the turn and gently pumped the brakes. My husband had thoroughly schooled me on what to do if this ever happened. But it was of no use. The minivan had a mind of its own. It came to life and was controlling our course like invisible hands on a Ouija board.

Kenny sang the refrain, which I echoed to the heavens above as I realized we were all at the mercy of the vehicle. The minivan was sliding across the center divider, spinning in slow motion. With a shock that felt like the zing from a stun gun, I realized there was a cliff edging the opposite side of the road. There was no fence, no guard rail, just a steep slope that looked bottomless. We were absolutely helpless.

I pumped the brakes more furiously. I cranked the steering wheel. I pulled the emergency brake. Nothing happened. We continued to spin in slow circles, working our way across the road. Doom's magnet was pulling us slowly toward the ravine, where we would be crushed to death. Nothing I did made any difference and there was nothing left to do that would make any difference. Then it occurred to me: there was one last thing I could do. I prayed.

As we circled around one more time to face the cliff, I saw it: the divine answer to my plea. About ten feet down off the side of the road and straight in front of us was a huge Douglas fir tree, tall and wide enough to stop a car in its tracks. I knew that if our minivan could land squarely in the middle of that tree, it would stop us from sliding any farther down the embankment. "Lord, please let us hit the tree. Lord, please let us hit the tree," I prayed with every fiber of my body. That magnificent tree could be our salvation, if only . . .

We had skidded completely across to the other side by now, and the front wheels of the van began their steep downhill descent. "Let us hit the tree. Please, Lord, let us hit the tree," I continued to chant. It was the only thing that would rescue us from certain death.

I could see a river coming into view at the bottom of the ravine, white water splashing over large boulders. Shock set in, and I was lured into a placid state where everything happened around me in slow motion. I was in the eye of a hurricane, the peaceful moment before drowning, and the quiet calm of acceptance at death's door.

Suddenly I awakened with a jolt as we slammed into that big beautiful fir tree. Hello, baby! I opened my eyes in astonishment. The hood ornament of my Dodge minivan rested squarely in the center of the tree. Bull's-eye!

A cry of relief escaped, and I immediately turned around to check the kids. They were still buckled safely in their car seats. "Don't cry, Mommy," Taylor reassured me, seeing the tears in my eyes. "We're okay!"

"Yes, you're right," I answered, my relief lasting only a quick moment. I realized the back end of the minivan was vertical. The drop was so steep that we were balancing precariously on the front two wheels. The slightest motion could tip us over, sending us crashing down the cliff. Even opening the car door could be the kiss of death. Had this been only a temporary respite? Did the tree stop our fall only to have the three of us freeze to death for fear of opening the car door and tumbling head over tail all the way down? The shock of this had just registered.

Out of the darkness someone yelled, "Unlock the tailgate!" I numbly obeyed.

As the back end lifted open, two men appeared and quickly removed my boys from their car seats. To this day, I can't figure out how they were able to do this without us tipping over. It seemed impossible.

They pulled me out, and I quickly scooped up the boys with relief, tears streaming down my face. The men helped us climb back up to the deserted road. No cars, no people, nothing but darkness as a black cloud obscured the moon. Where did these guys come from? I asked myself, but more pressing was the question of where do I take my boys now?

One of the men pointed. "See that house down the road? You'll be safe there, and you can call for help." I hadn't noticed it before, but sure enough, there was an old log cabin nestled in the woods not too far down the road.

"It's the house at Pooh Corner!" said Taylor, pointing.

"That's right," the man answered, smiling.

"Th-th-thank you," I managed to get out, and we began walking toward the soft yellow light on the cabin porch. "Mommy, who were those guys?" asked Taylor.

"Honey, those men were angels," I told him, and I looked to see where they had gone. You probably have already guessed. They had disappeared, not even leaving tracks in the snow.

California Dreamin'

Casey Pope

The California Trail, Carson Route, 1852

Sunny spring afternoon. A covered wagon being pulled by two oxen and heading east. In the distance, the Sierra Nevadas loomed. Sentries of California presiding over ingress and egress.

Calvin Inessa drove the wagon, a sluggish pace. His wife, Fair Inessa, walked alongside, keeping up without breaking a sweat. In her arms, a baby girl, to whom she was cooing.

Cal was twenty, but the coating of sunbaked weariness made him seem like an old thirty. Fair, on the other hand, appeared to have stopped aging from when she was fourteen years old, already four years past.

Fair, sensing Cal watching, looked up at him and parried his broody countenance with a brilliant smile, her best physical feature. Fair's teeth were preternaturally white and had the aesthetics of a Renaissance sculpture masterpiece. Cal returned her smile with a halfhearted effort. His teeth were nothing like Fair's. A chipped incisor, a missing canine, wheat-colored dinginess. He concluded smiling, focused on the trail.

Fair sighed and said to the baby, "Franny, your daddy is just an old stick-in-the-mud, isn't he?"

"I heard that," said Cal, low-grade snappish.

They encamped off-trail, next to a creek. Pitched the tent, started a campfire. As the sun was setting, the couple sat across from each other at the fire and ate their supper. The baby slept on a blanket nearby.

From the vast beyond came echoes of the coyotes' yips. Fair froze, looked over her shoulder, wide-eyed and frightened. Hustled over to Cal, snuggled up against him.

"Stop worrying," said Cal. "They aren't gonna bother you and me." He rubbed his chin in thought. "However, they do love the flesh of babies." Reacting to Fair's distraught stare, Cal chuckled.

The words blew out of Fair's mouth with furiousness. "Calvin Inessa! That is *not* amusing!"

"I was only funnin' with you."

"You are a bad father," said Fair, but only half-seriously.

"You know I'm not gonna let anything happen to you and Franny."

She harrumphed and gathered up Franny and said to Cal, "Kiss your daughter." He smooched the baby on the forehead. "Again, please," said Fair, and Cal complied. "Now kiss your wife." And he complied once more, but not on the forehead.

At first light, Fair was roused out of her sleep, the baby grumbling for the teat. Cal was not in the tent, and Fair poked her head out to check his whereabouts. And there he was in his skivvies, down at the creek, knee deep in it, shivering through a quick-wash routine.

When done, he stepped onto shore and immediately doubled over, clutching his midriff.

"Cal?"

"I'm all right," he said, but took another moment or two before he could stand upright. His abdomen displayed a two-inch gash from which stitches had recently been removed. The scar appeared less than amiable: weepy and angry.

Cal dawdled to the tent. Fair, with some attitude, threw a blanket at him. Ignoring her seemingly hostile presentation, he wrapped himself in the wooly warmth, kept his head down.

With raspy agitation, she said, "Why are you going in the water? The doc told you to keep the wound dry until it's healed."

Not backing down, he said, "Because I'm tired of stinkin', that's why."

"I'd rather have you stinking than dying."

"No one's gonna be dyin'."

Fair got up in his face. "Don't sass me, Cal." She tried to control her quivering lips, tears on the verge, but just could not. "I watched you get stabbed and bleed out like a stuck pig. And I thought for sure . . ." Cry-hiccups made her pause. "I thought for sure you were dead. I don't ever want to feel like that again."

She touched his shoulder, but he did not reciprocate and stepped back to gain some distance.

"Fair . . . We had a dream," he said, the tone resounding of accusation. "We had a plan."

"Is that what's been eating at you?" She made a noise, something like a grunt. "I knew it."

"*We* had a plan."

"Not if the plan means you dying over some bits of gold. San Francisco wasn't meant for us. The greed there almost got you killed."

"I could've handled it."

"I don't doubt that. But then you would've become a different Cal. You would've become one of them. I didn't want that to happen."

Fair walked to Cal and reached out to him again, and this time he did not back away. She tucked herself under the blanket, wrapping her arms around his torso, and his tensility slid off and pooled at his feet.

The baby started crying, and Fair looked toward the tent and said, "If nothing else, we got Franny from our time there. And that makes me not care about any amount of gold." She placed her palm on his cheek. "I know your pride's been hurt. But you can for sure be proud of being Franny's daddy."

Cal let out a sigh of resignation, and Fair made an exaggerated-stare face until he relented and cracked a wheat-colored smile.

"Mrs. Inessa," he said, "I do believe you have me wrapped around your little finger."

A big grin by Fair, her sculpture-quality teeth reflecting the morning sun. Up on tippy-toes to reach his face, she covered him with many kisses.

Oceanic expanse of the prairie. Blues skies abounded, dotted with cotton-ball clouds. The breeze roiling the endless grass and sagebrush. Fair stood on a small hill and squinted at the near distance. Her left hand shielded her eyes from the sun, while her right gripped the barrel of the rifle stood upright. Lifting the weapon, she held the aim for a three count and then fired.

Fair fast-walked to the target. She picked up the fat rabbit by its hind legs and placed it into the satchel hanging off her shoulder. In Fair's peripheral vision, a movement caught her eye and she turned her attention to it. A momentary hesitation; then she reached for the powder horn from the smaller satchel tied to her waist and poured the powder into the barrel of the rifle. She placed the patch over the barrel end, but dropped the ball into the grass. She was rushing.

"Slow down, girl," she told herself. She grabbed another ball, positioned it on the patch, knocked it in with the starter, and then took the ramrod and set the ball deep into the barrel. Cocked the hammer, placed the percussion cap, took aim.

She waited. She watched.

The figure on horseback approached. He wore an army uniform. Sat high in the saddle, an athletic lankiness to him. Likely in his late twenties.

"Good afternoon," said the soldier and raised his hands overhead in deference. "I am a lieutenant with the army, stationed out of Sutter's Fort. Please do not shoot."

Fair mulled the request as the soldier guided his horse closer. It wasn't until she could make out that his eyes were more green than blue that she lowered the rifle. They looked each other over, both unsmiling.

"I'm accompanying the army's surveyors. I heard shots, so I came to investigate." Eyeing Fair's brimming satchel of her catch, he said, "Looks like I have my answer. Are you with a party?"

Fair gave a curt nod. "I'm with my husband. Who also has a rifle. And will come looking for me if I don't return soon."

Unfazed by the insinuation, the soldier said, "Why isn't *he* doing the hunting?"

"I'm a better shot. *Way* better."

He coughed out a laugh. She let go a half-smile.

He said, "Are you two Argonauts?"

Another nod by her, less curt.

"Headed there or leaving?" asked the soldier.

"Leaving." She took a few seconds before saying, "It wasn't for us."

Staring deeply into her, he said, "Yes. I can see that."

Fair gave him a funny look. He kept staring, so she started talking.

"We're going to be homesteading instead. Cal, my husband, is not happy about it. He believes he's a failure, though I've told him otherwise."

The soldier said, "Life isn't always fair."

"That's what my daddy used to say."

"Wise man." The soldier removed his hat, backhand-wiped his damp brow, put the hat back on. "Well. It was a pleasure making your acquaintance." He turned the horse around and commenced heading back from whence he came.

"Lieutenant, wait," said Fair.

Abruptly reining the horse, he forced an about-face.

"I've been wondering," she said. "Why are gold seekers called Argonauts? Do you know?"

He smiled. "It's from a Greek myth. The hero, Jason, is tasked with retrieving the Golden Fleece. He assembles a team and they travel on a ship called the *Argo*."

The realization hit her immediately. "Oh!"

"That's right."

"Why did he have to get the Golden Fleece?"

"Jason's father, a king, was killed by the uncle when Jason was an infant. To save him from the same fate, the mother took Jason to a centaur who hid him away. When Jason grew up, he had to reclaim the Golden Fleece to resume his rightful position on the throne."

"Did he? Get the Golden Fleece?"

The soldier seemed conflicted about answering, but eventually said, "He did. But. The story ultimately ends in tragedy."

"Oh . . ."

"Because life isn't always fair."

They stared at each other contemplatively. Until, "Well, then, Argonaut. Be safe."

And with that, the solider rode off. Fair regarded him for a moment or two, then resumed chasing rabbits.

Fair approached the camp and saw two horses tied to the wagon. Stopping in her tracks, she scanned the site. A man was crouched at creekside, no shirt, rinsing off his torso. Another man was facedown by the wagon and motionless, his shirt soaked dark with blood. Fair focused on the prone man until his identity became clear. She folded over and gasped for air, clamping her hands over her mouth to avoid any sound escaping.

Her eyes frantically searched the grounds for—

Franny! Swaddled in a blanket next to the smoldering campfire. The baby squirmed some, but otherwise seemed unharmed.

With trembling hands, Fair started the process of loading the rifle, but she was hurrying, and the black powder went everywhere except into the barrel.

She whispered in a shaky voice, "Slow down, girl."

And she did. Deliberate step by deliberate step, she loaded the rifle and cocked it and aimed and marched toward the river. She could barely control her breathing, which came and went in rapid bursts.

The man stood and turned. He had a bleeding, knife-sliced gash across his chest. Seeing Fair, he raised an arm, shoulder level, palm out. "Now, hold on there, miss."

Fair pulled the trigger, and the ball slammed through the man's left pectoral and erupted out of the neighboring armpit. He stumbled backward, splashed into the water, shuddered twice, and went still.

Then another man's voice, quite belligerent. "Hey!"

Whipping around, Fair saw the other man sticking his fat head out of the wagon. No way could she reload the rifle in time. So she tossed it, rushed to Franny, scooped her up, and sprinted away toward the trail.

"Hey, dammit! Come back here," said the man.

"Oh God, oh God, oh God . . ."

Fair ran and ran and ran, but the man was on horseback. He came up beside her and bashed her head with a club.

Water was splashed onto Fair's face and she came to. She was on her back, lying close by the wagon, her hair matted and caked with dried blood. The man stood over her. Franny was crying, somewhere nearby.

Matter-of-factly the man said, "Tell me where you hid your gold or else I will gut your baby."

"Don't you touch her!"

"Tell me."

"We don't have any gold."

"Ain't no use lying. Your oxen's brand tells me you got them in Frisco. Now tell me where your gold is."

"We . . . We hardly had any to begin with. Spent what we had on the wagon and the animals and the supplies."

"All right," said the man. He walked to the wagon, and off the bench, he grasped the baby by the scruff and pointed a knife at her.

"No!" screeched Fair.

"Where. Is. The. Gold?"

Forced to panic-think, she blurted, "It's buried under the fire."

The man laid Franny back on the wagon bench, stabbed the knife into the wood surface beside her, went to his horse, grabbed a shovel, and tossed it to Fair.

"Start digging."

And so she did, but she bided her sweet time, her eyes racked with desperate concern over the fact that there truly was no gold. The man, fidgety with impatience, sat on the wagon bench and glared at her.

"Dig faster," he said. "And where's the whiskey? I need a goddamn drink."

"We don't have—" A flash in her eyes. Then, "It's, uh, in the chest, under the blankets, toward the bottom."

Through the canvas flaps, he entered the wagon and Fair darted to it, climbed up onto the bench, gripped the knife handle, and yanked. But the knife didn't budge. With both hands wrapped around the hilt, she furiously worked the knife back and forth. The blade creaked with friction against the wood until it finally came loose.

From inside the wagon, the man said, "There's no whiskey in here."

He stepped out of the wagon, onto the bench, and was surprised to see Fair there. He was even more surprised to see the knife handle sticking out of his upper thigh.

Fair clutched Franny, hopped off the wagon, and bolted away. The man slid the knife out and blood squirted into the air, a good three feet. He palmed the wound to no effect as the blood continued to gush out.

"Shit," he said, as if it were a minor inconvenience. He gave up on stanching the bleeding, unholstered his pistol, and shot at Fair.

The bullet entered her lower back and exited out of her belly. Her running faltered. But able to stay on her feet, she trudged on. Meanwhile, the man's blood flow slowed to a trickle, face gone pale, blank-eyed stare. He dropped the pistol and toppled off the wagon like a felled tree.

A weakened Fair was now on hands and knees. But nevertheless, she persisted, keeping forward momentum while holding a bawling Franny with one arm and giving her all to crawl away from the carnage.

The three-quarter moon lit the night-cloaked landscape. Fair hadn't gotten far before collapsing into a fetal position, a puddle of blood congealing beneath her. Franny was tucked tightly against Fair. The baby slept while Fair fought against doing the same. Every yip of the coyotes strengthened Fair's incentive to stay awake. But it was a struggle.

The coyotes closed in, and Fair heard growls and snuffling as they cautiously approached her. They sniffed her, nipped at her. She weakly batted at the animals, but they became emboldened with the knowledge that she was incapacitated and dying. The braver ones began tearing at her clothing. Fair balled herself up tight, cocooning Franny, a final effort to protect her baby.

Then. A gunshot. And another and another. The coyotes yelped and dispersed, panicked and agitated.

Fair opened her eyes and searched. Delirium-affected, and with blurred vision, she watched the centaur approach.

The soldier dismounted from his horse and knelt next to Fair. "Miss? Can you hear me?"

She asked in a desperate whisper, "Are you the centaur?"

"No."

"Are you the centaur?"

"Sure, yes."

"And you're here to save my baby."

The soldier examined her wounds and his disposition became that of no hope. He then checked on the baby. She wiggled and gurgled.

"Yes," he said. "I am here to save your baby. Miss? What is your name?"

"F-F-Fair."

"I know it's not fair. But can you tell me your name?"

Her eyes slowly closed.

"Can you at least tell me the name of your baby?"

She didn't answer. And he asked no more questions.

The moon sailed through the night sky and the soldier stayed by Fair's side until she died. By morning there were two dirt mounds with rudimentary grave markers for wife and husband. The coyote-ravaged bodies of the robbers were left to rot in plain view of the world.

The soldier guided the horse on an easy lope down the trail, intent on reaching the safe haven of Sutter's Fort at the heart of California. The baby was cradled in a satchel strapped snug against the soldier's torso.

"What am I supposed to call you?" the soldier asked the baby. He pretended to listen for a response. "What was that? Why don't I just give you a new name, you say? That would be a solution, I suppose. But if I name you, I'm responsible for you for the rest of my life. That's the rule." A heavy sigh by him. "So then the question becomes: Am I a man capable of that?"

The baby giggled.

"I appreciate your confidence in me, young lady. But I have to give it some thought."

The soldier came upon men he believed to be marauders, a band his fellow soldiers had been tasked to track down and contend with, and the likely progenitor of the two robbers who killed the Inessas.

They were about a hundred yards down the trail and headed the soldier's way. At that moment of reckoning, the soldier named the baby after her mother's last word. Because, as he explained, "Life is frequently not fair." Giving his now-presumptive daughter that name was a preemptive effort to stave off the inequities that the universe had to offer.

The soldier told her, "Your name is Fair. Let life treat you as such."

Unholstering his pistol, he aimed it with arm extended straight ahead and charged at the marauders. The soldier pushed his horse harder than ever before, and the horse gained speed until becoming a blur, reaching a velocity at which to outrun the Unfair Life.

Christmas in Santa Ana

Biff (Harold D.) Baker

He was on top of them before he knew it: golden cockroaches, as big as your thumb, shuffling around at the base of a tree in a raised sidewalk planter. A small crowd had gathered to watch, and they voiced their admiration in a blend of Spanish and English, which floated along the street. Clem stopped for a moment to observe the spectacle. He had seen the insects before, some time back. It had been a dark, warm night like this one, with air that clung to you like honey.

A young man in a hooded sweatshirt rattled by on a skateboard, weaving languorously, arms hanging straight down by his sides. Despite the new downtown with its restaurants and money, Clem thought, there were still a few blocks like these, wreathed in darkness, with an air of poetry, of mystery, enough for his needs. He liked to come here on weekend nights, at a safe distance from the leaden anxieties of his work. He came for that trace of mystery and to feel the movements of people around him.

Clem was well into his sixties. He had been married many years before, but that ended with wrenching inevitability. No other relationships followed, despite occasional clumsy attempts. His wife evolved into something startling and brilliant. He himself settled into the hardscrabble suburbs of this immigrant town, with Spanish-speaking neighbors who were friendly but busy with their families and jobs. Now he noticed, from the signs in shop windows, that Christmas was two days away. It had been some time since he'd received a present or needed to buy one.

At a short distance was a sidewalk memorial plastered on a utility box. A young woman had been killed on that spot. Clem studied the memorial. It showed a multitude of faces that were each cut in half, then recombined with half of another face to form a double portrait. In some cases there was resemblance between the two halves, in other cases none, but they all seemed happy, pleased to have been thrown into such random pairings. Clem found them disturbing. He saw himself being broken open and imagined it would be painful.

Ahead of him a knot of young people stood on the sidewalk outside a crowded hangout. As Clem approached, an incongruous figure forced her way through the middle of the group, although there was plenty of room to go around it. Clem watched the interloper with curiosity and dawning recognition. The woman's movements were hurried. As she rushed past him, she glanced quickly in his direction. He thought he heard a sudden gasp at that moment, though it did not come from her or from anyone else nearby.

She was a woman he had seen in the public library. The library was next to the Civic Center Mall, which for some years had been a sprawling encampment of the homeless. People from the mall filled the library's main reading room, especially when the weather was cold or wet. Clem came that day for the same reason as most of them, to pass the time. He had questions scribbled on index cards, and he prowled the library for answers. Its shelves were rich in unexpected discoveries, biographies of forgotten pop stars, obscure scientific inquiries, lurid fictions, lost or misunderstood episodes of history. That day he had found a novel about a Native American girl who changed husbands until her dwelling was full of beautiful children, all different from one another.

The woman sat opposite him, a couple of tables over, also occupied with her private study. She was flipping nervously through magazines and handwritten sheets of paper, as though at a loss for how or what to begin. A small rolling suitcase stood on the floor beside her. She was his age, with hair once brown but now almost completely gray, thick, pulled casually back from an unlined face with strong cheekbones and lips. It was a face from the old world, Clem thought. He wondered if she spoke with an accent, if she came from an educated family, a house with pictures and a piano. Her clothing was clean and neat and modest, even a bit stylish. What most captivated him was her throat. It was long and smooth and broadened into her shoulders, visible at the neck of her blouse. When she looked up, she had the amused, unseeing stare of one whose thoughts were far distant. He was sure she didn't notice him. At length she got up, gathered her things, and walked away. He waited in vain for her to return. That was weeks ago. It occurred to Clem that he had not stopped thinking about her, without ever being aware of it.

When he turned around, the figure had disappeared around a corner. He followed in the direction she had gone.

The street led to what passed for the city's gay district, with two bars and a tiny theater. He knew one of the bars and went there occasionally to chat with regulars. Clem was built dense and compact, deceptively like a boxer, though he had never been in a fight. Even his face was like a boxer's: rough and red, with a flat nose, as though battered. He had little sense of how others perceived him. Once he wondered if he were gay. It could have explained a lot, but the idea led nowhere. He just liked gay women and men, liked being in their world of easy humor and camaraderie. The bar was underground, connected to the sidewalk by a stairway. The doorkeeper sat inside, out of sight from the street.

Now, as he walked past the top of the stairway, a white Ford F-150 pickup came to a sudden stop at the curb. Clem noticed an American flag sticker on the side window. At that moment the street was empty except for the truck. Two young men in jeans and T-shirts jumped out of the cab and accosted him, one on either side. "Here's a fag," one said. Then, after getting a good look at Clem: "Hey, he's an old fag. Ain't no fag like an old fag, I always say." They grabbed his arms and swung him around, throwing his back painfully against the side of the truck. The men's movements were fast and sure, like farm-hands wrangling a calf. Clem tried to understand what was happening, but his mind was frozen by shock.

"How about you show me a good time, big guy? How about that?" One of them put his hands on Clem's shoulders and pushed down, wedging Clem's back hard against the rear fender of the truck. Clem, panicking, resisted the pressure, and they drew off to deliver a fast series of blows to his shoulders and sides. Finally, they jerked him forward onto his face and away from the truck. One of them bent over to say quietly, next to his ear: "We're makin' America great again. Tell the other fags we got their number." Then Clem heard the motor gun and the truck peel out. "Merry Christmas, asshole!" a voice shouted back as the truck moved off down the street.

Curled on the sidewalk, Clem heard steps and voices coming up the stairs. People from the bar, drawn by the noise, crowded up onto the sidewalk. Clem pushed himself into a sitting position. Hands touched him gently. "Jesus, are you okay? What happened? Hey, call nine-one-one. This guy just got attacked." He thanked them but declined their offers of help and rides home. When they pulled him to his feet, he felt shooting pains in his ribs. "Make sure you call the police and report this when you get home," one man urged him.

Clem did not respond. The vivid images of a few minutes before still hung about him: the white truck, the men's faces close to his, their grunts and curses as they worked him over, the smell of alcohol.

He wasn't headed home. He had other places to go. Something spoke to him clearly and insistently: the knight's move, ahead and to the side. It's there, all of it and more. Then, again, the sharp intake of breath sounded in his ears.

He looked around: the street was empty once more. Walking with difficulty, he continued to the end of the street, then hooked left to begin a complicated path back through the area. Clem had often walked this maze of darkened paths and alleys, but now he sought the labyrinth's center, the finished pattern of its long repetitions.

After a series of turns, he saw the woman standing some distance ahead, at the corner of one of the main downtown streets. He did not feel surprise, just a strange elation. She looked uncertain where to go, but as he hurried toward her, she started off to the right. When Clem came to the corner, she was lost from view, but he turned in the same direction and walked as quickly as his pains allowed.

By the time he emerged from the commercial zone into the grid of neighborhoods surrounding it, fatigue had nearly overwhelmed him. He stopped under a streetlight, then heard a voice behind his back. When he turned, he saw the woman face him from a few feet away.

"Are you looking for me?" she asked with a distinct accent. She was dressed the way he remembered her, in a light, long-sleeved top that showed her graceful neck and collarbone and loose-fitting trousers. He wondered if she had other clothes and how she kept these clean and new. She seemed older, but her dark brown eyes and brown-gray hair were the same. The fidelity of her image struck him like an unknown mercy.

"Are you looking for me?" she asked again, her voice and expression utterly serious. "No one comes looking for me," she continued. "Are you from the library?"

Clem did not answer the question, but asked her, "You speak with an accent. Where are you from?" She in turn let the question go unanswered. He tried again: "What is your name?"

The woman sighed and looked even more serious. "That's all gone, a long time ago. I don't remember that name. Now I have a secret name that I can't tell anyone."

Without thinking, Clem asked, "What if I guess it?"

"That's different," she conceded. "If you guess it, that's all right."

Clem waited a moment, then asked another question: "How did you come to live on the street?"

She broke into delighted laughter, her former seriousness dispelled. "It was easy! The easiest thing in the world." She stopped, looking into his eyes as though she found something there. "Come closer and I'll tell you." He came closer and felt her take his hand firmly. "Gravity," she whispered. "It's a simple law. If nothing holds you up, you go down." She laughed again, more quietly. "Now," she said, still holding his hand, "you have to guess my secret name. Don't let anyone hear you." Blind with happiness, Clem whispered into the ear she offered him. She smiled without responding. Then, letting go of his hand, she reached into her pocket and pulled out a piece of shiny metal. When she handed it to him, he saw it was a chrome insignia spelling "DustMaster" in cursive letters, obviously broken off of an old household appliance. "Carry this, so I know who you are," she said. "Take it to the library when you go." He looked down at the gift, overcome by the lightness that had invaded him.

At that moment a car appeared, approaching them from down the street, its stereo turned up loud, the bass line booming so strongly he could feel it all through his torso and groin. Clem watched the car, transfixed, unaware the woman had disappeared. It was a lowered 1969 Plymouth with tinted windows and custom paint. The vehicle stopped next to him at the intersection, pristine and glistening under the streetlights. From close up, he could hear the rough purr of its chrome exhausts under the pounding of the music. He noticed that the design was different from the usual metallic pinstriping of low-rider art. The longer he looked at it, the more he saw: across the hood and continuing over the roof and the surface of the trunk, there were landscapes, the white-peaked Sierra, the vast Mojave and Sonoran Deserts, Death Valley gleaming in colors like wet candy, the great Central Valley of California, and the harsh blue Pacific along a craggy shore. Above it was a dark sky with greater and lesser stars looking out through murky clouds. Now he saw structures on the land, and diminutive figures. But the light changed, and the car moved slowly off down the street, its thump-thump-thump fading gradually away until there was silence once more.

As he stood there, feeling the car's rhythm subside and the darkness of midnight penetrate its absence, another sound came faintly to his ears. He listened intently to what seemed the chaotic screaming of many voices. Then, as it grew louder, with fresh joy he recognized the source. It was the parrots! A feral colony, the legend said, spawned by birds who had escaped from a pet store delivery, or been released from a zoo during a fire—there were many versions of their story. Now they lived in the open, migrating about the region like a band of noisy, drunken vagrants. Wherever they came, at their unpredictable intervals, they brought the vision of unlimited space, of unlimited life, that Clem had glimpsed a moment ago on the car. The flock was settling out of the dark sky and into the trees overhead, flitting from branch to branch, tree to tree with frenetic, impatient movements. He stared up, unconsciously lifting his hands despite the burn in his side, trying to distinguish their large green forms. The din of their ceaseless cries just above and around him was deafening, so much so that, for several long minutes, surrounded by voices and wings, he thought of nothing, that is nothing at all, except the tale the night sang to him.

Earth Angel

Maddie Margarita

The moon was full when I rolled up in front of Ricardo's in my old, mostly ice-blue Chevelle Super Sport—the closest thing an ex-angel could find to flying on land. The temperature in San Juan had dropped to a balmy nighttime low of eighty-five degrees, and even with the top down I was sweating.

Birdie, my boss, certified shaman, and proprietress of the Hoochie Coochie—San Juan's "waxing salon to the stars"—had left me to fend for myself. Terrified to go home alone to my empty trailer on the beach, I'd hung from the reinforced hanging rod in the Coochie's storage room—by my ankles—then muscled open every can and jar in the employee fridge. I basically did what anyone who'd just found out they were the Knife Edge, a not-so-super hero fated to protect free will for all of mankind, would do. Rumor had it I was supposed to figure out how the Dark was breeching the mortal plane and stop it. But before I could do that, I had to find the man who'd started it all and convince him to help me.

Paralyzed behind my furry zebra steering wheel, I stared at the restaurant's stucco facade. I'd been here a hundred times, but never like
this. God, no, never like this. Tonight, the warm air was ripe with the
sweet goodness of corn tortillas, onions, and spicy mesquite-grilled
meat, and my stomach moaned longingly. I glanced up into the rear-
view mirror, fluffed my two-tone locks, smeared on a little bubble-
gum pink lip gloss for luck, and walked into Father Jack's favorite
place on earth.

Brilliant reds, blues, and yellows of the serapes jumped off the
walls. The Tejano beat pumped life into my chest. And for the first
time in my pre- and postangelic life, I understood why Father Jack
had loved this place so much. I also realized just how much I'd
missed—and dismissed—being an angel. It pissed me off.

Families occupied the tables. Loners lined the bar. I searched
the restaurant for Father Jack's familiar face. When it was clear he
wasn't here, I found a spot at the far end of the dark wood bar. There
was a mirror across from me, and I tried to keep my eyes on the door
in case that acid-spitting demon came looking for me again. Instead,
they kept shifting to the contented smile of a mother wiping the
messy little face of a beautiful baby girl.

"Cerveza?" the bartender asked.

I looked up at Lil Pain, and a long, silent whistle escaped my lips.

Jack's best friend had changed over the past five years. He now
had new, colorful tattoo sleeves, facial piercings, and deep crevices
around his brown eyes and full mouth.

Lil Pain took in my face and long strawberry-blond hair with dark
mahogany tips and frowned.

"Beer?" he ventured.

"Patrón Silver. No ice. No lime. No salt. And a grande chicken burrito with the works, por favor."

Pain gave me the grin that had launched a million confessions. "You don't order like a gringa."

I bared my teeth in what I hoped was a flirty smile then led with the truth. "I used to come here a lot, with Jack O'Shaughnessy." I grabbed a tortilla chip from a basket that belonged to the guy next to me.

"Don't think so, chica." "Lil" Pain wasn't little and didn't have to lean too far over the bar to check me out. "I woulda remembered you."

He pushed a glass of clear hellfire my way.

"Jack and I were closer than two people could ever be," I assured him, drowning my humiliation in tequila until the cords in my neck popped out. "And that's the God's honest truth."

"Still not buyin' it, baby girl." Lil Pain shook his head and expertly moved the chip bowl out of my reach. "You're not his type."

"Bullshit!" I yelled. Absolutely a little louder than I should've.

Of course I was Jack's type. The powers that be had matched us, picked me out of hundreds and thousands of angels to be his Guardian. I halted midthought. Why was that? Why out of all the angels in heaven had they picked me?

"Don't get me wrong, Mama," Pain purred. Smiling lazily, he took my hands in his. "That hair. Those green eyes. Those long legs of yours."

He glanced down the front of the black tank top I'd borrowed from the lost and found. "What I meant is you're more *my* type."

I stared at his flat, broad cheekbones, then into his warm, dark chocolate eyes, and suddenly couldn't feel my feet. I'd seen him work this magic from my angelic perch, but I'd had no idea what it felt like to be on the receiving end—until now. But the Lil Pain I knew would've cut off his arm before poaching a woman interested in his friend. Or maybe his bartender's instinct sensed trouble and he was kitty-blocking me, trying to protect his best friend.

But nobody kitty-blocked the Knife Edge.

I glanced nervously at the two lonely looking hoodie-wearing hombres down the bar. My transition from angel to a healthy twenty-three-year-old mortal woman hadn't exactly been easy. Especially where sex was concerned. Sure, I'd polished a few bats, cleaned a few balls, but nobody had slid into home—yet.

Partly because, for me, sex was an act of total trust where two people surrendered completely to each other, gave everything they had, took everything they wanted, and climaxed in the ultimate release of self. But mostly because where I came from, we thought the mortal sex act—and what it made people do—was absolutely, totally, freakin' hilarious, and whenever the opportunity arose, I couldn't stop laughing.

Sometimes just the thought of sex made me laugh. I bit back a grin and stroked the top of Pain's rough hand. "So, what is Jack's type?"

Lil Pain allowed his gaze to stray from mine and focused on someone or something over my shoulder. I knew her the minute I saw her at a table by the door. Blond, athletic, in a sheriff's uniform. The woman practically radiated goodness, and I had a sudden stabbing epiphany. Jack didn't even know I existed.

I quickly turned back around, but not before the blonde caught me staring and frowned when she noticed Pain holding my hand.

"Look," I said, more eager to get out of Dodge than ever. "I just need to talk to Jack. Please. Only he can help me. It's a matter of life and death."

He squinted. "You're not a cop, are you?"

"Do I look like a cop?" I demanded, realizing it might be harder to find Father Jack than I'd thought.

Lil Pain shook his head. "No. You look like someone who really needs what Jack's selling."

Jesus. I tried not to slide off the barstool. Was Jack dealing drugs? I felt sick to my stomach. It was my fault that he'd lost his soul, gone to jail, and gotten into whatever mess he was in.

"Please. I'm desperate," I told Pain, begging this time. "Can you just give me a number? E-mail? Address? Some way I can get in touch with him?"

Lil Pain turned his back and I watched him disappear into the kitchen along with any hope of finding Jack. He came back a few minutes later with my burrito and a note.

The Mission San Juan Capistrano. One hour.

I jumped on the brake with both feet in front of the Mission San Juan Capistrano, and the Chevelle smoked to a stop with three feet of rubber behind me. I couldn't do it. Relive the moment when I'd failed to stop Jack from killing that young pedophile in the confessional. Return to the place where I'd fallen from grace. Although, technically, Lucifer had *fallen* from grace. I'd been more dewinged and tossed out.

Heart pounding, I sat back and stuffed a stick of Juicy Fruit in my mouth—because demons hated Juicy Fruit—and nervously scanned the shops and restaurants around me for things that went bump in the night—then jumped out and ate you.

The mission's imposing red dome and brightly lit bell tower rose above the quaint downtown. Stunning in its simplicity, this jewel of the California missions was a place of power. A power that had felt benign the last time I was here. But tonight that same power set fire to the new black wing tattoos burning on my back.

I thought back to Lil Pain, the infinite darkness I'd seen behind his brown eyes and immediately regretted leaving those last few precious gulps of mind-numbing tequila on the bar. Not that it mattered now. There wasn't enough tequila in Southern California to blunt the stabbing pain in my head. And it only got worse the closer I got to the mission. By the time I pulled into the parking lot, my brain felt three times bigger than my skull and tears were streaming down my face. I dragged myself out of the car, staggered to the massive wood doors, and fell to my knees.

Jack appeared out of the shadows, a gray blur with a backpack, and my headache faded. Like whatever was torturing me had suddenly been shackled. He knelt next to me, not so gently lifted my chin, eyed my two-tone hair, then reached into his backpack and shoved a water bottle at me.

"Drink," he ordered.

No flash of recognition. No instant connection. I was semiprepared for that, but not for what came next. Father Jack's shiny jet-black hair was always meticulously cropped short above his clerical collar, and his translucent skin was marred only by premature wrinkles near his eyes—the price of carrying other people's burdens as his own.

But tonight, on the steps of the mission, Jack's long dark hair hung in silky waves just above the collar of his gray Dos Equis T-shirt. He had a two-day beard and his tanned face needed a shave, or a good wax. His straight nose and startlingly blue eyes were the same. But he seemed bigger and harder, and the mouth that once smiled easily was now set in a short, flat line.

I drank the bottle of water in loud gulps as Jack watched in silence. He obviously thought I was twerking, or tweaking, or whatever they called it. This was going even better than I planned.

"I'd like two oxy, three Ambien, and some heroin. Please." It came out sounding like a drunk run at Mickey D's and I shook my head. Why not just add an apple pie to my order?

"Is that what you think?" Jack demanded, like this was some sort of test. "That I am a damn drug dealer?"

"Uhhh . . . yes?"

Glaring at me, Jack pulled me to my feet, and I realized I had no idea who he was anymore.

He yanked me close until we were nose to nose.

"Did Luna put you up to this?" he demanded.

"Luna? I don't know any Luna," I swore, pretty much quaking in my boots.

Furious blue eyes bored into me for what seemed like a year. Then he pushed me away, grabbed his backpack, and took off for the parking lot.

I panicked. If Jack left now I might never find out if he could help me. And, honestly, I didn't want to do this alone.

"Wait." I ran after him, waving a handful of bills from my fanny pack. "I have cash."

Coyotes fueled by bloodlust yipped and howled in the nearby hills, and a slow ache crept into my chest. Maybe if I'd taken a few minutes between that run-in with that acid-spewing demon and becoming the Knife Edge to tidy up a bit. Brush my teeth . . .

But Jack wouldn't talk to me now. He wouldn't even slow down. And if he did, what if I said the wrong thing? Screwed the house cat once and for all?

The fate of mankind rested on my shoulders. It was heavier than you'd think.

Sweat puddled in my every crease and crevice. I rubbed at my temples. Being an angel had been easy. No decisions. No responsibility. Everything had been perfect. So clear-cut. So . . . pink.

Being human? All this free will? It was messy. Uncertain. Uncomfortable. But I was better than that now. I reached around and discreetly plucked a handful of damp leopard legging from my rear crevice. I was the Knife Edge.

I caught up with Jack and planted myself in front of him. I blinked.

He still had it. That stare. That gaze. That heady cocktail of passionate interest, distance, and "Whatever you're about to tell me, I've heard worse."

I tried to look away but two cool, clear blue lakes drew me in, rolled me, then pulled me weightlessly toward the cleansing fire of the abyss.

"Okay, okay!" I put up my hands in surrender. "I used to be an angel. At least until Raphael sliced off my wings and made me mortal. Now I work at the Hoochie Coochie. Ever heard of it? Waxing? No? Anyway, a demon attacked me this afternoon and my boss, a two-hundred-year-old shaman, announced I was the Knife Edge."

I yanked my tank top down to display the tattoo of the Earth precariously balanced on a blade, which had mysteriously appeared above my right breast.

Jack looked unconvinced.

"I don't want to scare you, but there are supernatural beings out there trying to stop me. If they find me they're going to kill me." I shivered.

Jack hesitated, then lifted a damp strand of hair off my cheek. "You're a mess."

I couldn't blame him. It was a lot to take in.

"Lil Pain was right to send you to me. I'm Jack."

"I know. I know," I said. "I'm Michaela. We need to hurry."

"Okay, Michaela." Jack put some distance between us and grabbed his backpack. "I have antipsychotics, generics at . . . uh . . . where I live . . . "

"Antipsychotics?" I glared at him in disbelief. "You think I'm crazy? You're crazy if you think I'm crazy." That sounded crazy. "I'm just having a bad day."

"It's going to be okay." Jack used his counselor voice and dug out a pen and paper. "Don't worry if you don't have a script. I can get what I need off an old medication container."

I grabbed his gray T-shirt with two hands—just above his nipples—to let him know I was serious. "There are supernatural creatures, demons, hellspawn, and God knows what else, out there just waiting to kill me. They've already tried at least once today. It's not safe here. We have to go. Now!" I jerked him close. "*Before* they unleash the hellhounds."

"You might need more than medication . . ."

"That's what I've been trying to tell you," I said, pulling him even closer. "I don't need medication. I need *you*."

He was about to make a run for it when a bat, or a flying monkey demon, swooped down on us and I collapsed into him. "I can't take any more today. Get me away from here. Please, anywhere! I don't care!"

"I know the perfect place," Jack said a little too quickly. "A place where you can get all the help you need. I'll get my bike."

His bike? Could this possibly get any worse?

Stricken, I dove into my fanny pack and held up my keys.

"I have a car." I pointed toward the Chevelle.

Centered in the halo of the brightest light in the parking lot, she shone a metallic glacier blue. Beige patches of Bondo on her back quarter-panel and hood only enhanced her natural beauty.

The grim line of Jack's mouth morphed into a half smile and he grabbed the keys. "I'll drive."

𝓕ilthy 𝓛ucre

Andrew R. Nixon

Barnard Levinson was class valedictorian of his private Cincinnati, Ohio, high school. Barnard, called Barry by his few friends and family, was also a classic, stereotypical nerd. Ink pens and mechanical pencils graced the vinyl insert of his shirt pocket. Adhesive tape wrapped around the center of his thick horn-rimmed glasses acted as a nonskid pad, keeping them from sliding down onto his nose. Still, he had a nervous habit of pushing the bridge of his glasses back up toward his bushy eyebrows, using his index finger. His too-short pants revealed ankles often graced with mismatched socks and occasionally mismatched shoes. Class bullies ignored Barnard. He was too easy a target.

During Barry's senior year of high school, he scored a perfect triple eight hundred on the college boards and was captain of his school's Technology Team. The dark brown coloring of the horn-rimmed eyeglass frames that adorned his face complemented his dark brown eyes, which were magnified by the thick lenses, thus earning him the nickname "Barney Google."

Though barely past his sixteenth birthday, his tightly curled close-cropped hair had already begun to recede, and flecks of silver hinted at his becoming prematurely gray. A crooked smile and uneven teeth could have been altered with braces, but the young man had no vanity about his appearance and refused to wear them. Barnard Levinson had the look of a tenured teacher instead of a young prodigy.

"Buddy boy," as his father called him, was preordained to become a mechanical engineer with a degree from the California Institute of Technology, like his dad had done. His teacher evaluations were golden. It was no surprise that Caltech, the only postsecondary school to which Barry had applied, offered him legacy admittance under the early-action admissions program.

Harrison "Harry" Scott was one of the first African Americans to attend the John D. O'Bryant Science and Technology High School in Roxbury, Massachusetts, where he excelled in the science curriculum designed especially for him by the high school counselor. When asked by his counselor why he chose computer science instead of pursuing medicine or law, Harry replied, "I know lots of black doctors and lawyers, but the only African American scientist I've ever seen on TV is Neil deGrasse Tyson. I want to be a scientist with my own TV show."

Harry scored very well on the college boards, missing a perfect 2400 score by two points, had solid teacher evaluations, and was granted early admission to both MIT and the California Institute of Technology. He hated the frozen tundra winters of Massachusetts. Although he could have commuted to MIT from his parents' home, Harry opted for the cross-country sunshine of Caltech's Pasadena campus. Had on-campus student housing not been a freshman requirement, Harry still would have opted to live in a dorm. He reasoned that on-campus student housing would afford him more library and lab time, allowing him to study instead of commuting to and from school.

An academic all-American, Harry was one of the most popular boys in his high school. His appearance was that of a rock star, but the only instrument Harrison Scott played was the computer. And he played it very well.

Harry's waist-long dreadlocks bounced above his head and trailed him, appearing to be a kite that followed him as he raced from class to class. His disarming smile and general mien reeked of enthusiasm. He could hardly wait to drink from the fountain of knowledge and college life at Caltech.

Class valedictorian Alario DePasquale, a first-generation American born to Italian immigrants who had settled in the foothills of Altadena, California, looked like a typical West Coast playboy. His olive skin and chiseled Roman countenance mirrored those of Michelangelo's *David*.

Alario's father, Anzio, had graduated from an exclusive technology university in Europe and had accepted a position with the Jet Propulsion Laboratory in Pasadena. Anzio led the NASA exploration team that placed the rover *Opportunity* on the surface of the planet Mars. On his desk, Alario proudly displayed the news clipping of his father that reads, "From its perch high in a ridge, NASA's Mars exploration rover *Opportunity* records an image of a Martian dust devil twisting through the valley below."

Anzio, a strong taskmaster, insisted his son keep his nose to the grindstone academically. Alario reluctantly studied hard, but bubbling just below the surface percolated a streak of wanderlust.

As a result of his natural ability and hard work in high school, Alario earned acceptance letters from Stanford, Harvard, MIT, and Caltech. The Italian-American engineer-to-be chose the latter. The freshman could have commuted the fifteen-minute drive from his parents' home to campus, but that plan was not an option according to school regulations.

The California Institute of Technology, unlike many other universities, requires that 100 percent of its freshmen live in one of the school's on-campus residence halls. Alario chose to live in the campus-approved Avery House facility, in a triple-occupancy dorm room, not knowing who his assigned roommates would be but trusting that they would have similar interests to his own.

Barnard Levinson and Harrison Scott received their official room and roommate assignments the same day. Both were assigned to the same Avery House dorm room. Their third roommate would be Alario DePasquale.

Kismet placed the three eager freshmen from different backgrounds together. Although their ethnic histories were as diverse as they could have been, all three had a common academic goal: to earn an engineering degree from one of the top technology schools in America.

The three college freshmen arrived on campus the same day, found their way to their home for the next four years, and became fast friends.

Many campuses include mild hazing of freshmen as a rite of passage, considering them as "the lowest form of life on a college campus" and engaging them in hijinks as an introduction to adult life. Not so at Caltech. Instead, freshmen are collegially introduced to extreme stunts and creativity for which the school has become legendary. In 1961 Caltech students altered the University of Washington's card stunts during the Rose Bowl to display "CALTECH." During the 1984 Rose Bowl game between UCLA and Illinois, the scoreboard was rewired to display Caltech trouncing MIT. In 1987 Caltech students changed the iconic Hollywood sign to read "CALTECH." More recently, at MIT's new-student orientation, heat-sensitive mugs were provided. When warm liquid was added, the moniker "MIT" became "CALTECH."

Upperclassmen wasted no time in welcoming the newbie residents of the triple, quickly eschewing their given names and calling them "Barry, Harry, and Larry," or collectively, "Nerd Cubed."

Fall semester freshman-year academics were a breeze for the three brilliant engineering roommates. They found their chemistry and physics classes to be just slightly more challenging than advanced placement and honors courses taken at their respective high schools. But calculus was a different story.

Their professor challenged the group, recognizing the potential of the unusual triplets. Professor Dimitri Ovechkin, a slender six-foot six-inch Russian immigrant, taught calculus with vigor. The first day of class, as the boys sat together, Larry slipped a note to his roommates that read, "Look at that guy's noggin. Reminds me of a chicken egg. I think we should rename him." Larry dubbed him "Dr. Ovum," not as a shortened version of his last name, but because his egg-shaped pate lacked a single follicle of hair.

Larry assigned funny and irreverent nicknames to each of their other professors, but the one that stuck was "Dr. Ovum." Of course, the boys would not dare use the name to his face. For that purpose, they addressed the professor by his widely accepted moniker on campus, "Dr. O."

The professor, as glib as his students, referred to the boys as "the Thinking Threesome," or occasionally as "the Three Amigos."

Study regimens were quickly established in the dormitory apartment. The three freshmen attended classes in the morning, studied briefly in the late afternoon, and had ample time for recreation in the evenings and on weekends. After one such study session Larry said to his roommates, "Gentlemen, I was reared in a strict Catholic home and one parable that was drilled into me began, 'Idle hands are the Devil's workshop.' Do you guys ever gamble?"

The conversation topic for that evening had little to do with academia. The three young men of the freshman class of the California Institute of Technology pondered life as they smoked a little weed in their dorm room. A blue-gray cloud that smelled like a mixture of damp urine and cold sweat permeated the room as each boy exhaled.

"Other than a few football and baseball pools, I haven't done much," gasped Barry in a falsetto voice as he held a roach using a pair of tweezers. "Never interested me."

Harry, who had been holding his breath, whooshed the tetrahydrocannabinol, and in a deep breath added, "I went to Jersey a few times. Played twenty-one and pretty much broke even."

Larry took a long drag on his joint, exhaled, and laughed. "Really? You broke even? That's what every liar says when he loses money. If breaking even was the standard, thriving casinos like Caesars Palace and the Bellagio would have gone bankrupt decades ago."

"Okay," responded Harry sheepishly, "I lost my ass. Why do you ask?"

"Well," continued Larry, "a couple buddies and I used to go to Primm, on the way to Vegas. It has a few small casinos, and they don't seem to check your ID as closely as they do in Vegas. It's only a couple hours' drive from here. I spent some time studying games and their odds and I believe that with a few tweaks we could develop my old system to beat the casinos. We would be doing what Ovum always preaches, 'putting our lessons to practical, real-life use.'"

"Cool!" said Harry. "I read that there are several Indian casinos nearby. We could try our luck there."

"I don't think so." Larry grinned. "We need a bigger, more anonymous place, like the joints in Vegas. We'd stand out at the smaller places."

Barry and Harry were impressed that Larry had called casinos "joints." It gave him an air of credibility. "But aren't we too young to go to a big-time casino? If we're able to sneak in the smaller places, why not stick to them?"

"Three reasons," began Larry. "Once we start to win, and we will win, the big places are less apt to hassle us. Second, the bigger the house, the more anonymous the gamblers. And third, regarding our ages, let's table that issue for the moment. We'll address it in a future agenda. For now, trust me."

With that, Nerd Cubed had a challenge, which they accepted with vigor. Barry, Harry, and Larry quickly began spending most of their evenings drinking, smoking, designing, and refining a system to beat the casinos in Las Vegas. Their motto became, "Design drunk. Refine sober."

They emptied a box that held reams of printer paper and stacked the contents in a corner, and each roommate tossed money into the box on a regular basis. They referred to the contents of the box as their "cash cache." The stash of gambling money grew as they designed and refined their system.

After their last class each day, the trio of skinny college teens stopped by the cafeteria and loaded up with nourishment for the evening's activities, or, as they called their snacks, "food for thought," working late into the night, like a trio of *Rain Man* savants.

The boys spent every night developing techniques to determine exactly when odds would be in their favor. One evening the logarithms lined up and all three marveled at the birth of a winning system. Harry examined the scheme closely while eating cold pizza and sipping a warm Coors Light. "Gentlemen, I've had an epiphany. Tonight we have graduated from the School of Creative Gaming. As of this moment we are no longer 'Nerd Cubed.' We are now the 'Wizards of Odds.'" His roommates nodded and applauded.

The rest of the fall term seemed to whiz by, and before they knew it they had completed their first-semester coursework and their scheme to beat the casinos was ready for a trial run during finals week. The boys could hardly wait to try it in a practical setting. The system had been tweaked and refined as much as could be done in a dorm room. It now needed to be tried in a casino.

Final-exam week was upon them. Classes were over for the semester and finals schedules posted. In a typical college setting one's exam schedule is dependent on the days and times of scheduled classes. Since the three freshmen had identical class schedules, all three would have the same testing schedule, staggered over two weeks. All their exams ended early Friday of the first week except the calculus final, scheduled for the following Monday. Barry, Harry, and Larry decided to use the weekend for a gambling run to Las Vegas. The sprint would serve as the boys' gambling final exam.

A week earlier, the Wizards of Odds boarded a bus and proceeded to a seedy section of South Pasadena, where they met a former Caltech student. Larry introduced Barry and Harry to the legendary "Computer Carl," notorious for making pristine computer replicas of driver's licenses and other forms of identification. His thriving business was especially attractive to underage students wanting to spend time receiving libation service in local pubs and other adult venues normally off-limits to underclassmen.

The National Minimum Drinking Age Act threatened to reduce federal highway funding by 10 percent for any state not adopting a minimum drinking age of twenty-one. For a fee, Carl provided an identification card showing the holder to be of legal age. The ersatz card was indistinguishable from a legitimate one. Three IDs from Computer Carl were purchased by the gambling trio.

Friday morning the boys rented a car and began the four-hour trip to Las Vegas. They planned to gamble through the weekend, or as long as the cash held out, and return early Monday morning in time for the 10:00 a.m. calculus final examination.

Upon their arrival in Las Vegas, they exited Interstate 15 at Tropicana Avenue and turned north on the famous Las Vegas Strip, passing the Bellagio and Caesar's Palace. Across from the Venetian, they spotted an erupting volcano that beckoned them. Driving around to the rear of the property, they parked the nondescript gray rental car deep inside the bowels of the self-parking lot. Barry, Harry, and Larry rolled their suitcases to the registration desk and checked into the Mirage Hotel and Casino, using the meticulously designed fake IDs that showed them to be several years beyond their actual age.

The hotel accommodations were nothing special. No problem. They did not plan to do much sleeping in the room, but used it to review each boy's role in the system. The plan was simple. Each Wizard would begin with a designated amount of cash and play until the amount was lost or doubled. He would then return to the room and wait for his comrades. Winnings would be kept in a separate box, but the original amount they had accumulated over the semester was invested. That way, once the entire original cache was gone, an easy calculation would show their winnings.

With the confidence of schoolboys on their first grown-up lark, the trio proceeded separately to the green felt tables and began to gamble. They gambled Friday afternoon and into the night, taking a break about two o'clock in the morning as planned. All three had either lost or doubled their grubstake by then. Returning to their room, they counted their winnings, reviewed the plan, and plotted their strategy for Saturday.

Luck for the young gamblers was up and down for most of Saturday and Sunday morning. They had planned to play out their last portion of money, win or lose, check out that afternoon, and return to campus in time for Dr. Ovum's calculus final exam. Instead they hit a winning streak that kept them at the tables throughout the night and into Monday morning. By noon they cashed in their chips, grabbed a few bites at the brunch buffet, and returned to the room with a substantial cache of cash for a much-needed rest.

Upon checkout, they discovered their room bill had been "comped," or picked up by the casino. Giddy over their good fortune at the tables, they left the hotel. The nondescript rental car was just as they'd left it. Tossing the suitcases stuffed with considerable winnings into the trunk of the rental car, the Great Triumvirate headed south on Interstate 15 toward Pasadena, a little after one o'clock Monday afternoon.

"Okay, guys, time for a reality check," began Barry, the most serious student of the troika. "We blew right through Ovum's final. I'm not about to have an F in calculus on my transcript ruin my GPA and jeopardize my scholarship. I mean, the money is nice, and we had a great time, but what do we do about the final?"

Larry offered a plan. "Let's tell him the truth. We went to Vegas and gambled and were on a roll and forgot about the time. He was young once. Don't you think he'd understand?"

"Why take the chance?" asked Harry. "We don't want to lie. So I say we offer a creative truth to the bald doctor."

"Meaning?" chimed Barry and Larry a cappella.

"We spin our tale," continued Harry. "We drove to Vegas and were having a good time. We were racing home late Sunday night in plenty of time to take his final . . ."

"And . . . ?" quizzed the two roommates in unison.

"And, uh, uh, the tire had a blowout in the middle of the desert. We weren't hurt, but realized the car had no spare tire or jack. Too late to call AAA on a Sunday, so we slept in the car, had the tire replaced this morning, grabbed some lunch, and voilà! Here we are for a makeup exam."

"Think he'll buy it?" asked Barry.

"Of course. Ovum is a reasonable egg."

"Okay, let's do it."

The three freshmen stashed the cash, returned the rental car, and went to the professor's office, arriving at dusk, just as he was leaving.

"So, what have you Three Amigos been up to that you missed my final exam?"

Harry, the spokesman for the group, told the prepared story in such a sincere fashion that Barry and Larry nearly had tears in their eyes. He ended the tale with, "So you see, sir, due to circumstances beyond our control, we just now arrived and beg you to consider giving us a makeup exam."

The wise old professor rubbed his bearded chin, thought for a moment, and in heavily accented Russian English asked, "Okay, gentlemen. You are prepared to take the exam right now?"

They all nodded, and Dr. Ovum led them to the classroom, where he slid his card key into the lock of the classroom door, opened it, flipped the light switch, and said, "Okay, Mr. Levinson, you sit at the desk in that corner, Mr. Scott, you in that corner, and Mr. DePasquale, you in that corner."

The boys winked and smiled at each other as they took their seats in opposite corners of the classroom.

The professor handed each a single sheet of paper. "Do you have something with which to write?"

The boys all nodded confidently.

"Very well. Please answer the following question." He took a deep breath, looked at each young man, and then went to the chalkboard and wrote, "Which tire?"

Full Service

Steven G. Jackson

Nobody came yesterday.

Day before, neither.

A feller came day before that, but just for water in the radiator. I couldn't very well charge him for that.

Pa called us a full-service station. And when Pa said full service, he meant it. No self-serve going on here. You need more 'n gas, we're your station. It's what makes us unique. One of a kind, to be sure.

It's hard making a living pumping gas out here in the California desert. We're the only business on this exit, so folks mostly ignore us. At least traffic on Highway 15 is steady. Lots of pricy rides, too. I call 'em *museum*-quality rides. Pa taught me to appreciate a special car.

Most folks stop down the hill in the big city of Baker. That's why our full service is so important. Otherwise we'd have to shut 'er down. Sis and I need to do right by Pa and keep it going, no matter what.

I'm told we're 'bout halfway between the cities of Lost Angels and Lost Vegas. I've got two rusted-out Vegas out back in what we called Pa's graveyard. They got to be forty years old if they're a day. I still don't get how you could just go and lose one. And then name a town after the ones you misplace? City folks is crazy.

I do understand the whole Lost Angels thing, though. It's easy for anyone to get lost in evil ways these days, even if you are trying to be mostly good.

I ain't been to either city. Farthest I've been is Baker. Pa and I walked all the way there once, before he passed. I could never live in a big city like Baker. Too many folks. Too much temptation. But they got A&W, so there's that.

Ma bailed when I was a boy. Pa said she couldn't stomach the family business. But I found a cross made of sticks out behind Pa's graveyard, and I'm pretty sure that's Ma down there. I didn't ever ask him 'bout it. Didn't seem like too smart a move, given his temper and all.

That's where Sis and I buried Pa, next to Ma. Sometimes the wind swirls extra hard right there. I think that's 'cause they're fighting down below. Then we started our own museum beyond the graveyard, so they won't be alone. The wind don't blow so much now.

That trip to Baker was when I first heard our station called the Graveyard by the competition. Pa said it was 'cause a the rusted-out trucks and cars out back. I don't know 'bout that. I think they was making fun of us. City folks can be mean.

But now we're proud to be called the Graveyard. It's who we are. Plus, we have something those city folks in Baker don't. Full service.

The sun will be going down soon. That cools it off a bunch. It's my favorite time a day. The desert sun angles down on Pa's graveyard, and everything's all shiny and red. You can see the heat shimmering off the cars and trucks. I cooked some grub on the hoods out there once, right by Ma and Pa. The company was nice, but the food came back all metal-tasting, and Sis threw it out. I didn't argue. Not with Sis. Pa didn't raise no fools.

I feel bad for Sis. She's got the same thing as Pa and me. Can't grow hair where you want it, too much of it where you don't. What's there is an oily, brown color that looks like someone puked in it. Our skin ain't no bargain, neither. Like moldy leather, 'cause of the sun. Maybe that's why she's awful quiet. Never sure what's going on in that noggin of hers. Truth is, she scares me.

Holy cow, somebody's getting off at our exit. A shiny black Aston Martin. Maybe we could chat for a spell. I miss that. Pa wasn't much of a talker, but he could listen just fine.

C'mon, baby. We've got gas, smokes, food, drinks. A fine selection, if you're not particular 'bout expiration dates. Lucky for us, most city folks don't notice.

Yup, they're getting out. Tall guy. Even taller 'n me. And that's tall. Short woman. Sis's height. Both way heavier 'n me and Sis. Both got shades, which is typical for these parts. I'm glad they're porky. The bigger they are, the more they eat and drink.

Hold on. The guy has a long overcoat. And he's wearing gloves. Uh-oh. In this heat, that can mean only one thing.

The wife wants full service.

"See that, Sis?"

She's behind the counter. Looks up from her *Cosmo*, gives 'em a stare, and then goes back to her dirty magazine. I'd say something 'bout damnation and all, but like I said, she scares me.

"Good," Sis says. "Cash is running low." That's a week's worth of words for Sis.

The man walks in first. He takes off his shades and scans the place, which takes only a sec. The woman keeps her shades on. She's fidgety. I can see a bruise behind those glasses.

"Howdy," I say, 'cause that's what I always say. Pa taught me good to be friendly, even if the folks ain't deserving. "How can we help you?"

The man is typical city folk. Doesn't smile. Nervous. I know the type. His first robbery. But he's been getting away with stuff his whole life, and he's sure he'll get away with this. "You really do full serve?"

"Yessir," I say, chest puffed out. "Only full-service station in these parts."

"What brand of gas is it? That's a high-performance engine out there."

It is, indeed.

"The premium's ninety-one octane. Just like down in Baker."

The woman is moving toward Sis. Sis don't pay her no mind, at least as far as a stranger can tell. But I know Sis is watching her like a hawk with that internal radar of hers. Sis don't miss nothing.

"Where you heading?" I ask, waiting for him to make his move. It's important he goes first.

Instead, he notices the video camera above Sis. "That on?"

"Afraid not. Stopped working years back. Ain't had the money to fix it. See how the recording light is off?"

The man thinks 'bout that. I don't know if they always believe me 'cause I sound honest, or look broke, or they just want to believe it so bad. Maybe city folks think I'm too stupid to make something like that up. Maybe a little of all four.

He makes up his mind, like they all do. Reaches behind his back, under his overcoat, and comes out with a gun. I recognize the kind from previous stickups, though I can't tell you the brand. He points it straight at me. "You fill it up with premium. Have the girl hand over the cash to my wife. Do as I say, and no one gets hurt."

Well, that's a lie. We've seen their faces, their car. It's not just 'bout robbery with him. This guy's decided to go straight from spouse abuse to killing.

No matter how many times this happens, I still get anxious. The guy does have a gun, and he means to use it. I don't think that makes me a coward.

"It'll work out better for you if you just leave now," I say. I don't really want him to, but the Christian thing is to give him a chance, and I feel obligated. Of course, I know he won't listen. In all my years of doing this, nobody's ever heeded that warning.

The man cocks the trigger. "I'm not afraid to use this."

No, I reckon he's not.

"Okay, mister," I say. "You win."

I put my hands high in the air and look at Sis, who still hasn't budged. That's her cue, and she pulls out her .357 Magnum. Blows a hole in his chest the size of a grapefruit. He never gets a shot off. Just like always.

We don't get that many full-service jobs a year. Just enough to keep us in business. Right after, it's always the same. The law takes a while to get there. It's always a different lawman, which I reckon is good. The morgue guy, he's always the same, but he doesn't say nothing, even if he's thinking it.

We all tell the same story. The video backs it up. Her husband came in, drew a gun, intending to rob us, probably kill us, and Sis acted in self-defense. We're all remorseful, and the law buys it. They're not much for long investigations out here. The wife is free to go.

They haul the body off, and the law is gone now. Just me, Sis, and the wife.

And the Aston Martin.

"How was the service?" I ask. We pride ourselves on satisfied customers.

She's been acting all sad for the law, but now she's smiling. "Perfect." She pulls out an envelope and hands it to Sis. "Your fee."

Sis counts it. She's not the trusting type. I don't blame her, but if it's short, there's not much to be done. It's not like we can ask for more later.

The wife wants to get out of here. They always do. She takes a few steps toward the door. "Thank you. You saved my life."

"How did you know 'bout our full service?" I ask, though there's only one answer. We don't use no Internet, or phones, or e-mail. Just word a mouth. It used to surprise me, how fast info travels. I guess when you're providing a service that's in demand, people find you.

She turns back. "My neighbor. Her husband abused her, too. She told me where to find you, how much you charge. How to dress my husband. What to have him do and say. It wasn't easy convincing him to rob you guys. I guess he just wasn't getting the same thrill out of beating on me."

I hear that a lot. City folks ain't never satisfied.

"One thing, before you go," I say. "Can I show you a for-real tourist attraction?"

"Out here?"

"Oh yeah. Come out back with me. We have an auto museum. It's worth a look."

She looks unsure, but follows me just the same. Sis brings up the rear.

There's dozens of rusted cars and trucks in the dirt behind the station. Pa's graveyard. The newer ones, the museum that Sis and I did, are over the hill. We've made some nice improvements. Like I said, worth a look.

"These look old," the wife says.

"I've got the newer ones over that ridge. A Ferrari. A Lamborghini. Two Rolls-Royces. All worthy of what Pa started." We walk over the hill, and a half-dozen models are sparkling in the last of the sunshine.

"Oh my," she says. "They're beautiful. Is that a McLaren?"

"Yup." One of 'em always gets their attention.

"It looks brand-new."

I feel pride in that. I polish 'em up every week. "It sure does. Ever sat in one?"

The wife picks up the pace. "Never."

The wife passes me and gets to the driver's window. There, she freezes. She turns back to me 'n' Sis, her hand covering her mouth. Her eyes are tearing up. "There's a decomposed body in the driver's seat." She loses her lunch. Just another mess I'll have to clean up. At least she missed the McLaren.

She steps away from us. "What is this?"

"I told you," I say. "Our auto museum."

"And the body behind the wheel?"

"Not my place to separate an owner from their car. This way they can keep Ma and Pa company." I point to an open spot next to a Bentley. "Your Aston Martin will go right there. I promise to take good care of it."

"You're stealing my car? And bringing my husband's dead body back here?"

City folks can be dumber 'n dirt.

"Not your husband. Too complicated."

She's panicked now. I get no joy out of that part. "You mean me?"

I don't answer. What's the point?

Now she's moved on to terrified. "But my neighbor. You didn't take her, or her car. Why me?"

"Her car weren't worthy. Only the finest get to be in the museum. Besides, if we took everybody, we'd get no word a mouth."

The wife shifts her attention to Sis, whose dead eyes show nothing. "You don't have to shoot me. You can keep the car."

"Oh, we ain't gonna shoot you," I say. "You can trace bullets."

I pull out some shackles from my back pocket. "We'll just lock you in your Aston Martin, and the sun will do the rest."

The wife blanches, which ain't easy out here in the blazing desert. "I can pay more," she pleads.

"Not necessary," I say. "It's all included in full service."

I Love California, Except for the Flakes

Wanda Green

Chapter 1

My toes felt like burning coals, my fingers were numb, and my back felt like someone had squeezed me between the prongs of crab-leg pliers to crack me open. I just stood there in the snow, trying to hold back my tears, afraid they would turn into icicles in this frigid weather.

I longed to be sipping on a strawberry margarita as I lay in the sun in the tropical setting of my sister's backyard in San Diego, California. But instead I stood in the utmost pain, trying to gather strength to ram the shovel into that mound of crap called snow. My hands kept losing grip on the shovel because I was losing strength and freezing.

Cold has no mercy, especially if you are friends with the Itis like I am. Cold is cruel to my friends tendinitis and bursitis, not to mention the abuse of my friend arthritis. The persistent joint pain, stiffness, and aching muscles made me wonder how I was ever foolish enough to lie down in this mess and sway my arms and legs back and forth to create perfect little snow angels.

I went inside to take a break and thaw out. I wanted to call my sister for comfort because she is the one person who could usually talk me off the ledge whenever I felt like I just couldn't take it anymore. But I couldn't handle her cheery, happy-go-lucky voice. I truly loved my sister, but I didn't want to hear how she and her friends were windsurfing or scuba diving in their pleasantly warm weather. Because I'd had enough torture for the day, I decided not to call.

It was time to go back into the freezing hell. If the wind stopped blowing, maybe I could have inhaled without my lungs turning into Popsicles. It was time to put on my sweater, hoodie, wool coat, snow boots, hat, scarf, and gloves to tackle the crap.

My mom came out of her bedroom, saw me looking like an over-stuffed burrito, and asked the same question she always asked. "Can I help you shovel some of that snow?" Without thinking, I screamed, "No, you can't!" I had to apologize for yelling, but she knew why I would never let her touch a shovel. It had been three years, but it felt like yesterday.

Three years ago, we'd had one of the most brutal blizzards ever. My hero, my dad, had a massive heart attack trying to shovel snow. Normally, it takes an ambulance five minutes to get to the house. Because of horrible road conditions, it took forty minutes. My mother's futile attempts to revive him didn't work. I believed if my mom and dad had lived in sunny California, he would still be alive.

For years my sister had begged our parents to move to California. My parents couldn't imagine living anywhere other than their hometown, where they'd grown up together, gotten married, raised a family, and where all of their friends lived. I'm the complete opposite. I tried to find a job in California for ten years. Every blistering-cold winter and every stifling humid summer were filled with searching for a job in California. I was persistent and determined to get there. Life is too short and I wanted to live it in a place where I knew I would be happy. I just loved California.

Chapter 2

Well, it finally happened. When I least expected it, I received an offer for a job in America's finest city—beautiful San Diego. My dreams had finally come true, and my endless nightmares of living on the East Coast were over. While I was screaming and jumping for joy, it suddenly hit me that I would never have to shovel snow another day of my life. I could lie out on the beach. I could go for long walks during the winter without a threat of frostbite. *Thank you, Lord.*

I just had to convince my mom to move with me.

My mom means the world to me. It's easy for her to say no about moving during an East Coast spring. When it's warm outside and you don't have cabin fever from being stuck in the house because of snow, it's hard to remember how miserable the snow can be.

I'd already lost one parent to snow and couldn't handle the thought of losing another. I didn't want to leave my mother, but I didn't want to miss the opportunity to live my dream in California. My sister and I pleaded with my mother to move with me. She refused. How would she manage without me during those ruthless East Coast winters? Would I get a call from the neighbor that they'd found her dead in the snow from a heart attack? Would she simply spend the entire winter indoors, sad, miserable, and lonely? While I always wanted the best for my mom, I had to start thinking about me for a change. I decided to hire landscapers who would take care of the snow for her, and a supermarket delivery service. All I could do was pray that she would change her mind after her first winter alone.

Chapter 3

From the moment the plane landed, I decided to hit the ground run-ning. I wanted to see and experience California from the farthest points north, south, east, and west.

I planned to live life to the fullest. The only thing that could stop me was time. When my time was up, I would stop. I love California. She is like my favorite auntie who always has a surprise or something sweet for me.

It was my first road trip as a true Californian. My niece had grad-uated from the University of California, Santa Cruz. The drive from San Diego to Santa Cruz was filled with breathtaking ocean views, rolling green hills, and layers of picturesque mountains. Santa Cruz forests were filled with the most beautiful and humongous redwood trees, which made you feel like you were in Alice's Wonderland.

The trip to the beach was filled with unexpected surprises. Although we did not see any signs stating it was a nude beach, folks were walking around wearing leaves and vines, and bikini bottoms without the tops. Santa Cruz is filled with people who have learned to appreciate and enjoy life.

As I was sitting in the bleachers waiting for the graduation to start, the lady next to me seemed to be getting increasingly agitated about something. Because I was so happy and excited to see my niece grad-uate, I couldn't help but wonder what was wrong with this woman. Everyone else around the stadium seemed very happy and excited with their balloons, flowers, signs of congratulations, and various other posters of accolades. *What could possibly irritate this woman so much that it would steal her joy on such an occasion?*

Every time she looked to her left at the bottom of the bleachers, she would sigh and give a look of total disgust. There was a young lady standing there wearing yellow bell-bottom pants, a large see-through flowered blouse, a pea-green fringed vest, and a rainbow bandana around her head with a little daisy neatly tucked behind her ear. The guy with his arm around her must have whispered something humorous in her ear. They would laugh and playfully hit each other as if they were having the time of their lives.

Watching them play and seemingly enjoy life would make the average person smile. That's why I couldn't understand why this woman was so irritated. Her endless sighs were really getting on my nerves.

I was finally going to be at one of my niece's commencements. I'd missed her preschool, middle school, and high school graduations, but I wasn't going to miss this one. I was so happy that I would be able to spend time with my niece without a countdown clock ticking in my head of when I would have to fly back to the East Coast.

I finally turned to the woman and politely asked, "How are you today?" She must have interpreted the question as, *You must tell all your business to a complete stranger.* She began by telling me how her son drives her nuts. She angrily pointed. "Look at him down there. He has a carefree life, where he does whatever he wants, however he wants. He comes out of the house looking and acting like a clown."

Just as she said that, he started dancing. He held his nose with one hand and did a jerking swim stroke with the other. Suddenly, he started shaking and frolicking around like a fish out of water. His girlfriend starting dancing and then motioning as if she were gently swimming through smooth waters.

"Young people don't dress by the same rules that we had growing up," I said to lighten the conversation, and tried not to laugh at the show the young couple put on.

With tight lips, she shook her head and said, "He is so silly and disrespectful. He goes into my closet and grabs whatever he wants and wears it. As a matter of fact, the dress he is wearing is one of my favorites. Why would he wear that at his sister's graduation? His sister and girlfriend thinks he looks cool." She crossed her arms so tight that I thought she might break them like a crumbling pretzel.

I asked if she was upset because he was wearing her favorite dress or because he was wearing a dress. In response she just continued to complain about all the occasions when he would wear various items from her closet. This discussion was stirring up anger instead of dissolving it.

I tried to think of something to say to change the subject, when she explained that his whole attitude about life had changed after his father died. Of course, that got my attention. I didn't feel like going into the whole story of my dad's death, although I did clutch his wedding ring, which was dangling from my gold necklace. I decided to just give her my opinion regarding her son. I told her I believed that after his father died, her son had realized life is short.

"But what does that have to do with wearing my clothes? He won't even buy his own dresses."

I explained. "I believe he is enjoying life and trying to keep his one parent, who is still alive, close to him at all times. Clothes have taken on a new meaning. He knows that his mother's clothes look like her and smell like her. I believe he is most comfortable when he is as close as possible to her. He obviously loves his mother and would hate to lose her."

Her demeanor began to change. She unfolded her arms and began to slowly rub her legs back and forth. "I never thought about it that way," she said in a humble voice.

Because she was listening to me, I continued. "If it was just about wearing women's clothes, he would buy his own. Wearing his mother's clothes is like having her loving arms wrapped around him."

This really made me start to miss my mom.

The woman took in one deep breath as a tear fell from her cheek.

I told her that he is in Santa Cruz, where everyone is a little different, carefree and doing their own thing. "It's not a matter of whether you will see a man in a dress; it's a matter of whether you will see a man in a dress that looks better than yours."

She smiled and thanked me.

My sister leaned over to the woman. "Isn't this a beautiful day for a graduation?"

"It most certainly is," replied the woman.

Chapter 4

Since living in California, whenever my sister said "let's," I said "go." Spending time with my sister was a dream come true. One thing I had to get used to was sharing my sister with her friends. I will not call them strange or creepy because that's not nice.

Instead, I would just say they were special. Two of her friends always planned excursions for all of us to go on. The trips to the wineries were fine, but the trips to the haunted places in San Diego are simply unnecessary. Their strange obsession with death and murder mysteries threw me for a loop.

On one outing, we would go to the beautiful botanical gardens or the history museums in Balboa Park, and then the next excursion we would go to some crazy place, like the desert at dusk, where there were snakes and scorpions.

They suggested going for a walk, which turned into a rigorous hike. We ended up at Potato Chip Rock on Mount Woodson Summit. The hike was up to a big rock that had a very thin ledge sticking out of it that looks like a huge potato chip. The chip was so thin that it didn't seem able to hold the weight of an infant—much less a grown woman. "Go ahead and climb up on the chip to really see the view," they insisted.

I really think they just wanted to see me fall to my death. After all, they were special and loved death. The view was beautiful, but not to die for.

The mud pools were another excursion. Bubbling pools of mud in a big field popped as you walked by. All I could think of was quicksand. But my sister and her special friends were fascinated. I was just praying and watching my every step, making sure I didn't sink to my death.

As much as I want to live life to the fullest, I had to draw the line when they suggested that we go snorkeling with leopard sharks. They insisted that it would be the experience of a lifetime. If I had a bucket list, snorkeling with sharks would not be on it.

For months I suggested that we could go to the orchards up in the mountains, to pick apples and enjoy some delicious apple pie. Finally, we were on our way. It was in December, so there wouldn't be any apples to pick, but it would still be a beautiful place to visit.

I decided to take a nap on the way. As usual, my sister was asleep five minutes after we started driving. Although it was a little difficult to sleep while hearing discussions about mysteries and death, I managed to finally doze off.

I woke up when I heard one of them ask, "Did you bring the chains?"

I knew it. These death freaks were planning to kill me.

I didn't open my eyes because I wanted to hear their plans and let them think I was still asleep. They kept going back and forth discussing if they should use the chains or if they even needed them.

I couldn't take it anymore, so I opened my eyes ready to attack before they could attack me, when I saw it. It was everywhere. I couldn't believe what my eyes were seeing. My heart starting racing and my hands were shaking. I saw it floating through the air like it was supposed to be there. *But we are still in California. How can this be?* I just started crying out, "Nooooo, noooo, noooo!" My sister woke up, and everyone asked what was wrong. With tears in my eyes, I whispered, "I see snowflakes."

Just for Fun

Glenda Brown Rynn

Ben finally spotted his little brother in the Mammoth Mountain Ski Lodge cafeteria. With his red ski jacket stuffed under his left arm, he was lifting a yellow tray from a stack onto the slider grill.

Huh, hardly a little brother, Ben thought. Garrett had topped out at six foot four, towering over Ben's five eleven. Ben wove his way through the assorted skiers in yellow, red, orange, silver, black, and multicolored jackets as they talked and laughed over lunch with family members and friends. Outside on the deck, their skis and poles stood propped against the open wooden fencing, as if staying vigilant for signs of avalanches on the surrounding white hills and mountains.

Garrett, looking over the salads, hadn't yet seen Ben.

Hmmm, thought Ben. *I'm a little early. Haha, I'll surprise him.*

Ignoring the two male skiers who were stepping over to the line after Garrett, Ben quick-stepped to Garrett's broad back, drew back his arm, and then rammed his knuckles into the middle of Garrett's gray sweater.

"Stick 'em up!"

Garrett's yellow tray flipped into the air. He whirled around, his big eyes popping. The lady on the other side of the salads screamed, and the two men next in line gasped. For one instant Ben looked up into Garrett's blues, which were assessing his attacker as his fists readied themselves.

In the next instant, Ben was bashed by two yellow trays, one to his head, the other on his shoulder as the two skiers shouted and leaped forward, smashing him to the floor while slugging.

"Help! Help!" screamed the salad lady.

Garrett yelled, "Ben!" as he doubled over to wrangle up his brother. Others in the café scrambled to the commotion and surrounded them. Then two security guards materialized, their hands on the guns at their hips.

An hour later, the two frowning security guards escorted Ben back up from the security office below and released him. Ben sheepishly surveyed this main level for his brother, avoiding the livid or fearful eyes of those few skiers left who had seen the earlier ruckus. Those fresh from the highway or the slopes busied themselves around the food and coffee.

Garrett, sitting in a corner, waved a long arm at him. Through the large window by his brother's table, Ben saw skiers scattered across the white slopes, like ants exploring a new area. Ben waved back but then pointed to the cafeteria counter and indicated he'd get his lunch and join his brother.

As he passed the desserts, he took a piece of apple pie and then motioned a food attendant over. "Do you possibly have any chocolate cake?" *Garrett's favorite.* Yes, the worker said, one was just coming out of the oven. Ben asked the man to take a large piece, when ready, to the big man sitting at that corner table and pointed. "I'll pay for it."

He smiled to himself. *Chocolate always helps.* He put a hand up to the knot on his forehead. *Ugh. Still sore.*

Ben paid at the cash register and explained about the piece of chocolate cake he'd ordered. Avoiding eye contact with those scattered skiers who were nudging each other and motioning at him, he sorted his way to his brother's table, sat down, and stuffed his ski jacket and hat onto the chair to his side.

For a few seconds their eyes locked as he sat, mute. Both disgust and amusement emanated from Garrett's blue eyes.

"Yeah, I know," Ben said, ducking his head. "It was *stupid*." He paused. "But a special piece of chocolate cake is coming your way, part of my apology." He pointed a finger back toward the cafeteria line.

Garrett scowled. "Why did you *do* that?" His bushy black hair flopped across his forehead as he leaned forward with his forearms on the table, his gray turtleneck sweater taut with his muscular build.

Ben shrugged. "Oh, just for fun."

"Man, we haven't seen each other for four months, make a plan to meet and ski together, and you almost wind up in jail!" Garrett threw his hands up.

"Well, it *did* cost me two hundred dollars, if that makes you feel better." Ben chomped into his hamburger.

Garrett snorted but shook his head. "You're *lucky*. Do you know that?"

"Yeah, I know. But how've you been?"

Staring down at his finished lunch, Garrett breathed heavily, working to switch moods. Then he nodded slightly. "Things are looking good. Just got a generous raise." His eyebrows wiggled above his blues.

Someone was approaching the table on Ben's left. A young woman held forward a dish with a large piece of chocolate cake. She smiled at Garrett, her brown eyes bright above her yellow spandex top where MAMMOTH was printed in black across her breasts. "This is for someone here."

"His." Ben pointed to Garrett. "A present from me."

"Aren't you lucky." Cocking her head at him, she batted her two-inch eyelashes. "Are you a birthday boy?"

"Not today." Garrett chuckled, gazing upward, amused at her coy attitude. The laugh lines by his mouth and eyes crinkled once again.

Ben's nostrils flared. His younger brother had always been the chick magnet. Ben unclenched his teeth and lifted an eyebrow at his brother. "You want the cake on your right or your left?"

Glancing quickly at both sides of his finished lunch plate, Garrett sat up, paused, and then firmly said, "The right side."

The woman slid the plate onto the table and elegantly presented Garrett with the extra fork she'd brought as if a token of her admiration. She inclined her head at him. "Call me if you want something. Okay?"

He flicked his palm at her. "You betcha."

She turned to leave but shot one last smile over her shoulder at Garrett. Ben thought, *Mammoth babe didn't even look at me.*

Garrett forked a large wedge into his mouth. "M-m-m. Delish. Thanks, Big Bro."

"Looks like you finally got right and left figured out. Congratulations."

Clunk. Garrett dropped his fork onto the table. "For God's sake, Ben. Haven't we left that childhood crap behind?"

Ben shrugged. "Just sayin'."

Garrett sat rigidly. "Yes, yes, yes, I did. I'm okay now." His expression was stoic. "But I still have nightmares about other kids in school whacking me on the back and laughing every time I held up the wrong hand."

Ben felt a grin take over his face.

Garrett pointed a finger at Ben. "And especially about that day Mrs. Morrison kept me in at recess and drilled me with the correct ways. When I came home, you and Sis got in my face, swore she was mixed up, and hammered me again that my left was right and right was left."

"She and I were just six and seven when we got that idea." He tried to straighten his face. "We didn't realize."

"Doesn't matter if you were seven or seventy. I bet it was your idea." Garrett's eyes narrowed. "Why did you do that to me?"

Ben lifted his shoulders. "Well, just . . . for . . . fun."

"Oh, *fun* again. It damn sure wasn't fun when I realized I couldn't play team sports."

Ben breathed deeply. "C'mon, Bro, you lettered in swimming and track. And those are teams." He stuck out his jaw.

"Yeah, but not like football or basketball."

Heat flushed across Ben's face. "Well, that's better than me. You're twenty-eight now. Looks like that old confusion is gone."

Garrett snapped. "Yes, finally! Except when I'm taken by surprise or afraid." *Wham!* Garrett whopped the table with his fingers. "This conversation is officially over. Let's go skiing. Grab your things." Garrett stuffed the last piece of chocolate cake into his mouth, jerked his ski jacket and black knitted cap off the chair next to his, and stomped away.

Ben pulled on his orange and brown jacket and followed.

With their skis balanced on their shoulders, they caught up on each other's recent activities as they trudged their way through children playing in the lower snow and skiers headed for the different lifts.

At the three-seat lift line, they found themselves behind twin sisters whose blond curls wiggled under white caps onto the shoulders of their puffy pink jackets, a contrast to their black leggings. The twentysomethings introduced themselves, bragging and giggling how they had recently finished advanced lessons, but maybe they could ski on the intermediate slopes.

Garrett turned to Ben. "Let's plan to be back down at the lodge no later than four thirty. Okay? Besides that"—he pointed up—"it's beginning to cloud up."

"That's fine. Four thirty." Ben nodded with an upward glance.

When an open chairlift swung around for them, one of the twins tugged on Garrett's red jacket. "C'mon, catch this one with us."

Ben watched the pink twins lift off with his red brother between them. *Shit. Why isn't it me in that chair?*

Then he looked behind him to see who his lift companions would be. On the alert stood two men in their fifties, one tall with a bushy beard and wearing a black jacket and the other about five foot two and wearing a yellow jacket. *I'll be riding with Blackbeard and Shorty, not Pinkie and Winkie,* Ben thought.

When the next chairlift swung around, Ben plopped on the right end, Blackbeard slid in on the other end, and Shorty scrambled for the middle. Ben pulled the safety bar down. The lift swung over the ground and then up into the air. *Whew.* Ben sighed, as did his seatmates, who began talking. Up ahead, Garrett and the Pinkies were motioning around to the mountainside and its sights below. A few drops of snow were beginning to fall. Mixed in with them, Ben smelled marijuana smoke wafting back from a chair farther ahead. He partially unzipped his jacket and dug his hand within.

A moment or two later Ben deeply inhaled the first drag on his joint, held it as long as he could, and then blew it out slowly. Shorty jerked in his seat and growled to Blackbeard, "Oh no, we've got a pothead here." Blackbeard groaned.

Ben snapped, "It's legal!" The other two rolled their eyes and muttered to each other.

"Don't you have any consideration for others?" Shorty snarled.

"You've got mountain air here, stupid. Breathe it." Ben set his jaw before taking another puff.

Snow sprinkles blew all around them as the lift continued. Up ahead, Ben could make out where the landing would be. On his side, the ground snow looked fairly close to where the bottom of the lift paused but then slanted steeply down on the left.

As the lift neared the stopping place, Ben and the two others readied themselves to disembark. He and long-legged Blackbeard hit the ground on each side at almost the same time, but Shorty was still wriggling to the front edge of the seat. Ben shuffled one ski, yelled, "Oh no," waved a ski pole, and threw his left hip against the outside of the chairlift, making the lift jerk sideways. Shorty fell flat onto the edge of the platform. As the lift swung away and another one drew closer, Shorty, slithering to the left, wound up sliding down six feet of snow, some on his face. A few gasps came from scattered skiers and those on the incoming lift before Blackbeard could help him. Ben guffawed and then turned to where Garrett and the pink sisters waited several yards to the right.

Shorty's voice rang out. "I'll get you for that, pothead!"

Smirking to himself, Ben skied away.

He skied with Garrett and the twins over the next hour. Although the snowfall was still light, Ben found it easy to see into the distance. Both twins had individual falls and even one small collision with each other, but amid laughs, Ben and Garrett helped them back up. The slopes were busy with skiers zipping down, trying to beat the sun slipping behind the summit.

After concentrating on a long downhill swoop, Ben looked back up the hill but didn't see Garrett's red jacket anywhere, nor the Pinkies.

Oh well, he'd just ski by himself for a while—although other skiers were on the move.

A number of moguls and one fall later, Ben held his gloved hand over his goggles to block the snow and studied his watch—four o'clock. Better start heading closer to the lower center of the mountain. At that moment the sun dropped just behind the summit. The snowfall liked that omen and increased. He studied the direction he needed. *Hm-m-m,* a few rock outcroppings and farther down a few trees to the east. Everything had turned gray.

Ben sighed, made his tired body get it together, and aimed his skis in the direction of the lodge in the steady light snow.

Boy, a hot cup of coffee, here I come.

He lifted his goggles for a second and squinted below to the east. That red jacket—and a pink one to the left. Must be Garrett and one of the twins. *Ha! I should zip down and get between them.* He adjusted his goggles and pushed off.

A sudden sluicing noise to his left startled him. Snow sprayed from a racing ball of yellow power that cut a diagonal across his path a few inches from his skis, knocking his ski pole out of his hand.

"BREATHE, STUPID!" a crouched Shorty yelled, quickly disappearing.

Thrown backward, Ben struggled to balance himself. *Where's Blackbeard?* Ben twisted left as much as he dared, trying to spot Blackbeard coming behind Shorty.

But a few seconds later a black tornado whammed against the back of his right shoulder, pushing his arm up. The ski pole went flying. The tornado yelled, "Pothead!" crossed to the left, and headed for oblivion.

Ben flipped and flailed this way and that, trying to balance as he skied backward a couple of yards before he could straighten out. *My poles. I need my poles!*

Bending his knees sharply, he hovered over his skis with his arms far out like a hawk as he erratically shaved mogul after mogul. Then his skis sped into a smoother patch. Before he could catch his breath, his head screamed *ICE!*

His speed doubled as he careened over the long, glistening patch. At its end, he tried to jump the edge back onto the snow. The front of his skis plowed through three inches of built-up snow, but he managed to break through without falling.

Still wobbly, Ben was approaching Garrett's broad back but going faster than his brother. Pinky, about ten yards away from Big Red, would soon be nearing those jutting rocks on her side.

I gotta go around, Bro. "On your right!" Ben yelled.

His brother wobbled and his head turned slightly as if he was trying to hear better.

Oh God. Is he mixed up? Ben took a deep breath. "NO, on your left!"

The big red jacket and black trousers jerked a few inches to one side and then to the other.

"NO, NO, on your right!" Flailing his arms, Ben used all his strength, aiming his skis past Garrett on the right—as his brother's body and the cluster of pine and fir trees that way grew larger.

Garrett bent his knees sharply, and his form began to swoop to the right.

"NO, NO, LEFT!" Ben screamed. *I gotta pass him. I gotta pass him.* He leaned to the right until his trajectory could overcome his brother's.

One of his waving arms knocked his goggles askew. He whipped his hand up to straighten them.

Ben screamed, "NO, Noooooooooooooo! NO-O-O-O-O-O! The TREE-E-E-E-E! The TR—"

The Kick the Bucket Tour

Jo Perry

The light turned red while the driver regaled her passengers with details of Ramon Novarro's torture murder. That's why the roofless matte black van belonging to Kick the Bucket Tour lurched so late from Laurel Canyon, where Novarro lived, into the tangle of westbound traffic on Sunset and forced a motorcycle cop to swerve into the next lane.

"Those familiar with the grisly murder scene report that Novarro's ghost still haunts the property."

Oops, the driver thinks, regarding the cop. I just massively fucked up.

The driver tilts her oversized Afro-wig-haloed head, blows a lip-glossed I'm-so-sorry kiss at the cop, and then purrs into her mic, "And here, folks, is a member of the famous LAPD!"

The sun-scorched, jet-lagged, disoriented tourists wave obligingly at the grim-faced officer.

"Never say I don't love you," the driver coos. "Ain't no mountain high enough, baby!"

The cop waves and then guns it up Sunset.

The tourists laugh.

They'll laugh at fucking anything, the driver thinks, remembering to arrange her mouth into a smile.

I was wrong about the stupid Diana Ross costume the tour now required, she thinks. It works. So does Ramon Novarro. What the hell is wrong with them? Can't they tell when they're being played? And don't people get murdered or off themselves wherever the fuck they live?

The driver slides the van into a no-parking zone, emergency lights flashing.

"On your left is 8024 Sunset Boulevard, once Schwab's Pharmacy, where Lana Turner was discovered." Lana Turner was discovered downing a soda at the Top Hat Café, but whenever she doesn't say "Schwab's," a passenger "corrects" her.

"And on your right, the infamous Chateau Marmont"—the driver compensates for the way the speakers slur her words by overenunciating—"designed by William Douglas Lee in 1929 and modeled on an actual royal château in the Loire Valley of France."

The passengers gape at the actual faux château.

The driver glances at the tip jar, empty except for the five one-dollar bills she put there herself, and at the bottles of water and container of hard candies she purchased with a maxed-out credit card and to which she's invited the van's guests to help themselves.

"Do any of you wonderful folks know who kicked the bucket at the Chateau Marmont?"

"F. Scott Fitzgerald?" a woman offers. The woman is so fat that her flesh appears to melt from her small head and pool around her massive red ankles.

"Close—really close!" The driver shuts one heavily mascaraed and false-eyelashed eye into a game-show wink. "Are you by any chance a librarian, ma'am?"

The fat woman nods.

"A librarian, I knew it! And where are you from, ma'am?"

"Wichita, Kansas."

"Let's hear it for librarians and for Kansas!" the driver says and then waits for the idiotic clapping to subside.

She gets three or four librarians a week. They all love homicides and gore.

"F. Scott Fitzgerald almost died here," the driver offers. "He had a heart attack at the hotel. And a heart attack killed him a year later not far from here on Laurel Avenue in West Hollywood. You might say Hollywood broke his heart."

The tourists shift in their seats. They don't care about deaths from natural causes. That's not why they paid sixty-five bucks to Kick the Bucket Tour.

"Comedian John Belushi died of a massive overdose in a Chateau bungalow on March fifth, 1982, after Cathy Evelyn Smith injected him repeatedly with a mixture of heroin and cocaine called a 'speedball.'"

The driver silently counts to three and then utters, "What a waste of a hugely talented life."

The tourists squint into the blistering, white-hot afternoon, conjuring the victim's final moments and contemplating the senseless but somehow satisfying cruelty and horror of his demise.

The speedball always shuts them up. Now what?

A twinge traverses the right lower quadrant of the driver's belly.

I'm not getting my period early, am I? Great. Just great.

As car after car refuses to let the van enter the surging traffic, the driver touches the iPad on the seat, which causes the theme from *The Blues Brothers* to blast across the van.

Then, recalling what her boss told her just this morning about "guests" complaining that she played too much music, she mutes the soundtrack.

"Lots of other juicy things have occurred at this outré Hollywood landmark," she says. "James Dean jumped through one of the hotel windows during his audition for *Rebel without a Cause* . . ."

Approving murmurs.

"And rumor has it that Dennis Hopper hosted orgies on the hotel premises"—the driver pauses while titters ripple through the group. "No wonder they have soundproof walls. Too bad they're so strong, though—famed director Helmut Newton died after crashing his car into the hotel."

A sudden opening and the driver jerks the van onto Sunset, almost flattening a homeless woman pushing a mutt in a baby stroller across Marmont Lane.

The driver is not herself today.

Maybe it's the Santa Ana winds slicing fronds from the palms, overturning trash cans and gusting so oven-hot that the driver's wig has gone from itching to scalding.

Yet the resolute driver powers onward, transporting her charges from one lurid-death locale to another until the melted silver mirages over which she navigates threaten to engulf her and the van.

"Welcome to 722 North Elm Drive, ladies and gentlemen."

The tourists stare at the huge Spanish-style house, which looks almost exactly like the other Spanish-style mansions nearby.

"Did you know that this peaceful-looking home, the ill-fated Menendez family's opulent estate, was previously owned by none other than Elton John?"

Why did I say "none other"? I sound like an ass. Get it together, girl, she tells herself.

"Or that their horrific murders were so incredibly violent that Kitty's and Joe's bodies were unrecognizable?"

Gasps all around.

Good.

One of these days I'm just going to drive to random houses and make shit up, the driver promises herself. I'll invent horrific murders of people who never existed. How much you want to bet that no one will even know the difference?

She's been working the murder-suicide tour for six months now, and besides being a total happiness-sucking downer, it's changed her. Even the bustling afternoon Trader Joe's parking lot feels like the scene of a rape-murder to her. Every tree is a suicide tree. Every wavering shadow, a killer.

The traffic is horrendous. Was there an accident?

There's always an accident.

But the tourists use the slowdowns to refresh their sunscreen or to help themselves to water and candy as they, like diners between sumptuous courses, contentedly await the next thrilling intimation of mortality.

Finally—a fatal collision between a delivery truck and a motorcyclist has caused a nasty bottleneck—the van rolls to a dignified stop across from a row of nondescript houses.

"Welcome to 3831 South Norton Avenue. Perhaps the darkest place in the dark and murderous dark heart of Los Angeles."

Oohs.

"The place where the grotesquely posed body of the young and beautiful Elizabeth Short, also known as the Black Dahlia, was discovered by an unsuspecting housewife on a sunny January morning in 1947."

Was it sunny? Cloudy? Maybe there was a fucking tornado. Who gives a shit?

"Her fiendish and savage killer has never been found," the driver says, hinting that the surgically adept psycho killer will hop aboard to murder and pose them all any second now.

Another strategic pause, then, "Did you know the victim had been surgically bisected and that all the blood had been drained from her body?"

Aahs.

The blood thing. Always a hit.

As the driver steers toward Koreatown, the ache behind her forehead blooms into a massive premenstrual migraine, and the twinge morphs into abdominal cramping.

"Thirty-four hundred Wilshire. The glamorous Mediterranean and Art Deco Ambassador Hotel and Cocoanut Grove nightclub, the site of six Academy Award ceremonies and the spot where Hollywood's greatest stars performed and hung out. Robert Kennedy was tragically shot and killed here in June 1968. The hotel closed in 1989 and was demolished in 2006. The pantry where Kennedy was shot, however, was deconstructed and is now kept in storage."

The tourists ogle the brutalist modern school buildings now occupying the site.

"Sirhan Sirhan was Kennedy's killer, but witnesses reported seeing a man and a woman in a polka-dot dress running from the hotel kitchen." Pause. "Who were they? Were they involved with Kennedy's assassination? No one knows."

A few murmurs. Nothing more. Shit.

She's got to do better. Keep the shocks coming.

A seething wind burst rakes the passengers' heads and parches the driver's throat as she rehashes Peg Entwistle's suicide by hanging from the Hollywood sign's *H*, George Reeves's Benedict Canyon suicide—or murder, Natalie Wood's drowning, Marvin Gaye's death at the hands of his father, Bob Crane's bludgeoning, the shooting of Rebecca Schaeffer, the severed head of Bronson Canyon, Phil

Hartman's murder, Haing Ngor's Chinatown execution, and the grotesque death of Canadian tourist Elisa Lam, whose body was found in the Cecil Hotel's rooftop water tank.

"How did Elisa Lam's body find its way into the tank?" the driver intones.

Maybe she'd fucking had it, the driver thinks. Maybe she threw herself in.

The van glides past the white-walled 12305 5th Helena Drive, where Marilyn Monroe overdosed, past the Petersen Automotive Museum on Wilshire where the Notorious B.I.G. was gunned down.

The black van proceeds west, then north.

"Eight ten Linden Drive, where mobster Bugsy Siegel was murdered. Four fatal shots were fired that night in 1947, one of which blew an eye right out of Siegel's head."

Gasps.

Then 1527 Benedict Canyon.

"Speaking of mobsters, this is where mob daughter and writer Susan Berman died in a gangland-style hit allegedly at the hands of her best friend, Robert Durst."

A few coughs.

These lumps aren't interested in Susan Berman or "allegedly" anything, the driver realizes. Durst maybe—the cross-dressing thing is good—but not his not-beautiful and not-rich victim.

The iPad plays "Dead Man's Curve" as the driver describes the lethal stretch of Mulholland Drive memorialized by Jan & Dean.

I'd murder for a latte and a pee, she thinks. I have that Laugh Factory audition tonight, too. Why tonight? When I feel like crap? When I look like shit?

The driver is actually quite attractive. Beautiful, even. And hers is a pretty solid stand-up routine, the usual fish-out-of-water, Midwestern black girl comes to LA schtick—but she's worked in some good jokes about the murder tour that make it fresh.

The driver halts at a stop sign when the heat or lack of humidity or a mysterious and malignant force bears down on her until she can hardly breathe.

Something has to happen, she thinks. Or else. Something big.

She's exhausted the inheritance she'd received when her childless aunt died. She's behind on the rent of her studio apartment, and the tour pays only minimum wage plus tips. Forget eating.

If I don't make it soon, the driver realizes, if I don't score an improv gig or steady atmosphere work on a network show, I'll end up like those crazy losers selling selfies in Hollywood.

She could go home.

A tear accompanies the thought, sliding down her cheekbone and taking blush with it, then evaporating before it reaches her chin.

Returning to Springfield would mean defeat, would demonstrate that she was nothing special, no different from the people she hauled around in the van, would prove that her intuition that her destiny was something astonishing was just an illusion.

That she would never be famous.

And she needed to be famous.

Fuck it, she thinks then. Fuck the Hillside Stranglers. Fuck Whitney Houston, Bonnie Lee Bakley. Fuck Fatty Arbuckle and fuck the tourists.

The driver wills her lungs to suck in a long, cleansing breath.

She exhales and reminds herself, Today is the first day of the rest of my life. Then she urges the van forward and activates *Diana Ross' Greatest Hits*.

I believe in you, her inner voice insists. Someday everyone will know who you are.

Reinvigorated, the driver croons into the mic, "We've arrived at 3301 Waverly Drive, the site of one of the Manson family's most demonic and gruesome murders."

She'd used "horrific" before, but while flossing her teeth this morning, "demonic" popped into her head.

So much better!

"Leno and Rosemary LaBianca. Leno was a supermarket executive. Rosemary owned a dress shop. On August 10, 1969, former homecoming queen and Manson follower Leslie Van Houten held Rosemary down as Tex Watson stabbed her husband. Then Van Houten and Patricia Krenwinkel stabbed Rosemary more than fourteen times."

Awed silence.

The tourists are still quiet when the van arrives on South Bundy Drive.

"Nicole Brown Simpson. Ron Goldman," the driver announces. "The notorious 875 South Bundy Drive—or it used to be. New owners have changed the infamous street number to 879."

The driver gives the passengers time to absorb this information and then says, "Did you know that Nicole's feet had no blood on them? And that this told detectives that she was the first to die?"

"Oh my God," a passenger says.

Then another. "Oh my God."

They're ready.

Ready for what the driver calls "dessert."

Although it violates chronological order and geographical sense, it is the culmination of all that had come before. It is the complete package: a deranged, sadistic, senseless, tragic, gruesome fatal violation of a young and beautiful woman.

The driver steers the van up Benedict Canyon, then onto Cielo Drive, moving toward a steep, unmarked gated private road.

The driver announces, "10050 Cielo Drive. Cary Grant, Henry Fonda, Terry Melcher, Candice Bergen, and Roman Polanski and his wife, Sharon Tate, once lived beyond this very gate."

Very?

"A day prior to the LaBianca murders, the Mansons took five lives here: twenty-six-year-old actress Sharon Tate and her unborn child, heiress Abigail Folger, hairstylist Jay Sebring, writer Wojciech Frykowski, and Steven Parent, the unlucky friend of the gardener."

Sighs.

"Although Manson ordered the murders, Tex Watson, Susan Atkins, and Patricia Krenwinkel committed the grisly and horrifying homicides, which involved slashing, stabbing, cutting, and shooting. Hardened police investigators were shocked by the bloodbath."

Murmurs.

"The night of the killings, Watson climbed the telephone pole and cut the line. There would be no way the victims could call for help." Pause. "The first to die was Parent, shot and stabbed by Watson as he approached the house.

"Inside the cursed residence, Folger was stabbed twenty-eight times, Frykowski fifty-one."

Gasps.

"Tate pleaded for her life to no avail. And after the brutal killings, as Manson directed, the killers wrote 'Pig' in blood on the door."

The passengers slouch in stupefied silence, meditating on fate's cruelty and the fragility of life.

The black van somberly descends the brittle hills, coming to rest like a battered ship at Hollywood and Vine, where a crush of unemployed actors impersonating celebrities and comic book figures jockey for poses with tourists.

"Thanks to all of you fabulous people for choosing Kick the Bucket Tour!" The driver smiles and bats her fake eyelashes. "Tell your friends! I'd be grateful for a five-star rating when you visit our website, and remind you that tips are appreciated!"

The driver gets out, revealing six-inch heels and the flared pants of her sparkly, slinky purple Diana Ross costume. She slides the van's door open, cautioning passengers to watch their step as they exit onto the sticky pavement.

A few thank the driver.

A couple stuff dollar bills or pocket change in the tip jar.

As the fat librarian struggles to step down, a muscular Spider-Man charges forward. "Selfie with Spider-Man? Only five bucks."

"Not now." The driver raises her hand as if to swat him away.

The librarian achieves the curb just as Spider-Man removes something from his fanny pack and hurls himself forward.

Then he thrusts a long knife into the driver's chest.

Spider-Man efficiently and repeatedly stabs the driver until blood marinates the front of her costume and drenches the sleeves.

The librarian and a few remaining passengers watch.

"Please," the driver begs as the figure shoves the weapon into her left breast, then bows and melts into the crowd flowing toward Ripley's Believe It or Not! museum.

A passenger inserts two fingers in his mouth and whistles his approval.

"Wow. Just wow," the librarian says and begins to clap.

The applause is tepid at first, then swells as the driver collapses—her world going black and cold and silent.

The driver, a handsome young aspiring actor dressed as Charlie Chaplin, delivers his vanload of tourists to the final stop, a sticky patch of Hollywood Boulevard not far from Grauman's Chinese Theater and across the street from the Ripley's Believe It or Not! museum.

"And this, folks, is the end of the line." Dramatic pause. "As it was so tragically for one of our very own Kick the Bucket Tour guides just a year ago, savagely knifed to death on this very spot by a deranged man."

Gasps.

Good, he thinks.

That works every time.

Life Dies, and Then You Suck

Steven G. Jackson

December 18, 1974—Woodlawn Cemetery, the Bronx, New York City

I hardly expected to be disturbed as midnight struck in the poorly lit cemetery. But as luck would have it—mine, not so much his—a young man in a heavy black coat stepped up to me as I gazed down at Millicent's grave. My Milly. I was the only one allowed to call her that.

"You a fan?" the man asked. He had a reporter's ID pinned to his lapel. Some second-rate rag. Certainly not one of mine.

I chose my words carefully. I didn't like to lie. After decades of getting everything you want, you lose the compulsion. "I loved her very much."

The man squinted at me. "I know the light's awful out here, but you look a lot like the old man. Are you related? Her son, perhaps?"

"Yes and no."

"Well, what is it, man? If you're related, there's a free drink in it for you before the bars close."

My eyes bored into his, freezing him. "Since you asked, I will tell you a story." I searched his face for comprehension, but found none. "Then I will have that drink.

"It is common knowledge that I left Hearst Castle, or 'La Cuesta Encantada,' as I referred to it, for good in 1947, when my health forced me to vacate for medical care unavailable locally. When I 'died' in 1951 in Beverly Hills, I left a publishing and art empire to my five sons, who continue to thrive, much to my gratification. I was interred in the family mausoleum at the Cypress Lawn Cemetery in Colma, California. That's my official story, and I'm sticking to it.'"

The breeze kicked up. It must have been uncomfortable for my guest, but my gaze kept him in place, so he'd just have to endure. Me, I felt nothing. "But as my father taught me, it's always the story within the story that's important to dig up." I laughed. "*Dig up*. After 111 years, I still haven't lost my wit."

I recalled with a certain degree of conflict my final days, and my redemption. If that's actually a thing. I used to think so, but now I'm not so sure.

"On my last night in San Simeon, everyone around me knew I was dying. But not everyone had given up."

October 20, 1947—Hearst Castle, San Simeon, California

"Polly," I called out in a voice barely above a whisper. "Is my garlic soup ready?"

Polly Graf entered my bedroom with a bowl and a straw. "Coming, Mr. Hearst." Polly was a stout woman, with brown hair and a frown that could burn toast. Her "chief-of-staff" uniform fit tightly. "Barbie is bringing your wine."

I took the bowl and grunted. "A sure sign I'm about to kick the bucket. Eating through a straw because my teeth all fell out. It won't be long, Ms. Graf, before you inherit the Casa del Monte."

Polly couldn't hide her excitement at the thought, though, in hindsight, she probably should have. The Casa del Monte was my least favorite of the three guesthouses on the property and the one Polly and her daughter had lived in since the girl's birth. That allowed me to save my favorites for the rich and famous guests I used to be able to host.

"The legend of William Randolph Hearst will live forever," Polly said. "You have built a wonderful legacy."

"How long have you managed the staff here?" I asked.

"Twenty years, sir. It's been an honor to serve you. Loved every minute of it."

My hearing wasn't so good, but I still managed to catch her whispering to herself. "Now hurry up and die, old man. So I can inherit what's mine."

Before I could remind her of her place, her teenage daughter, Barbie Dahl Graf, carried in a glass of red wine and put it on my nightstand. She was as thin as her mother was stout, and her black hair was cut short. "Here's your wine, Mr. Hearst."

"Thank you, my dear. Red wine is my last civilized indulgence. What do we say to the doctors who disapprove?"

"We say 'too bad,'" Barbie replied. She shifted her attention to her mother. "I overheard you, Mom. You want someone to die?"

Polly's eyes gave away her fear at being caught. "Of course not, dear. You must have misunderstood."

Barbie frowned, and I chose to let it go. When you have only a few breaths left, you get pretty particular about when to use them.

There was a knock on the door.

I perked up. "That must be Linda. Please show her in."

Polly escorted my hospice nurse, Linda Hand, into the room. If Polly was too thick and Barbie too thin, Linda was just right. Now in her fifties, she had California beach-blond hair that showed signs of her age with twists of gray.

She rushed to me. "How are you feeling today?"

"Your arrival always cheers me up."

She gave me a long hug. "I'm sorry I'm late. I picked up a special order for you."

"No worries. I'm not going anywhere. Besides, Polly and Barbie take good care of me."

Linda glared at Polly, who sneered. But Polly saw Barbie watching her and switched to a smile.

"I have an amazing surprise," Linda said. "A cure!"

"A cure for Mr. Hearst?" Barbie exclaimed. "That's awesome!"

Polly didn't look so pleased. "Yes. Awesome."

I appreciated Linda's effort, but knew my condition was hopeless. "Linda, you know my many diseases have no cure."

"That's right," Polly said. "You shouldn't give him false hope."

Linda checked my pulse. "You have such soft skin."

Polly looked incredulous. "Seriously?"

I laughed. "My skin is like filo dough. I think you're confusing translucent for soft."

But Linda was undeterred. "And your eyes. So gentle. When you're back on your feet, we'll go dancing."

"Dancing?" I said. "I think you've been dipping into my medical stash. Maybe hitting the reefer my doctor recommended. My kidneys don't work." I saw Polly smile from the corner of my eye. "My liver is failing." Polly pumped her fist. "My arteries are so clogged, blood moves like a California traffic jam at rush hour."

Polly raised her arms. All she needed was someone to high five. Barbie, Linda, and I stared at her.

"Mother," Barbie said, "why are you happy Mr. Hearst is sick? He's always taken care of us. Now it's our job to take care of him."

Polly rushed to her daughter. "Of course it is. I just had a muscle spasm. You believe me, don't you?"

"Sometimes adults are confusing," Barbie said. "They say they'll do something, but then they do something else. My psych teacher says people do that because they can fool some of the people all of the time and all of the people some of the time. And that's enough to keep them lying."

Polly patted her daughter on the head and then turned back to Linda. "Can we get back on topic? Ms. Hand, what's this nonsense about a cure?"

Linda pulled out a vial of red liquid. "It's not nonsense. It's the cure. An unorthodox one, but it's my job to save him, and I will."

"It's your job to make him comfortable while he dies," Polly said. "And I'm certain that isn't on his approved prescription list."

"True," Linda said. "But it is the cure."

"You're giving him false hope," Polly said. "You're just after his money."

"I think she's trying to save him," Barbie said. "I think she's a heroine."

I waved for them to stop bickering. "Stop it, all of you. Linda, I can't take that. You could lose your license."

"I don't care," Linda said. "Just drink this, and you'll be better soon."

"What if it kills him?" Polly asked. After a moment's thought, she smiled. "Never mind. Carry on."

"Mother!" Barbie said. "I'm so mad at you right now."

"What's in it?" I asked. "Stem cells?"

"Sort of," Linda replied.

"Where'd you get it?" I asked.

"I ordered it from the Transylvania underground," Linda said.

Barbie perked up. "Underground? Like for criminals and illegal stuff?"

Linda nodded. "It's the only place you can order this. Short of flying to Eastern Europe and picking it up yourself."

I fondly recalled some childhood trips. "My parents took me all over Eastern Europe as a child. A superstitious pair, they were. Came to believe in all the local folklore."

"Do you believe?" Linda asked.

"In what?" I answered.

Linda stared at the vial. "The legends of those cultures. In particular, vampires."

Barbie rushed to the bed. "Vampires? Cool."

"Oh, come on," Polly said.

Linda held up the vial. "This is vampire blood. Enough to turn you."

Polly reached for it. "Sir, you can't drink that."

But Linda held her off. "Because it might work? You might lose your precious guesthouse?"

Conflicting thoughts raced through my brain. "I don't know, Linda. I don't really want to be a vampire."

Linda pulled out a second vial. "I'll go with you. We can be a couple."

Barbie put her hand over her heart. "That's so romantic."

But I was horrified. "No! You've got your whole life in front of you. I won't let you ruin it."

Linda pouted, but put the second vial away. "Then you drink it. At least I can save you."

I took the vial, paused, and then, without truly thinking about the ramifications, swallowed it. "Ooh, that's strong." I smacked my lips. "Tastes like chicken."

"Do you feel different?" Linda asked.

I *did*. "Something. Hard to describe. I feel a little—" A sudden rush of pain forced me to grab my chest. I fell back on the bed.

Linda rushed in and checked my pulse. "He's gone."

"Hallelujah," Polly said.

Barbie took my hand. "Mother!"

"Don't you see?" Polly said. "This is best for everybody. He's out of his misery. And we get to live in Casa del Monte forever."

"I really thought it would work," Linda said.

That's when I exhaled and then sat up.

"You've *got* to be kidding me," Polly said.

"William!" Linda yelled. "You're alive!"

I was pretty sure that was an exaggeration. "Alive? Not so much. But I feel marvelous!"

Linda hugged me. "It worked! Now you'll get to live in your estate forever!"

Polly glared at her. "Oh, bite me."

I looked at the pulsing carotid artery running across Polly's throat. "Trust me, there's nothing I'd rather do." I smacked my lips. "But I still have no teeth. What's up with that?"

Polly's eyes grew wide with a newly formed fear. "You can keep your guesthouse. I quit. Come on, Barbie."

"And miss this?" Barbie said. "Are you nuts?"

Polly backpedaled, then froze and made a cross with her fingers. I gave her a quizzical look and then laughed.

Meanwhile, Barbie stepped back and checked her hair in the mirror—and noticed I had no reflection. "Mr. Hearst, you're invisible!"

I followed her gaze and looked into the mirror, which shattered harmlessly. "Sorry about that. Occupational hazard." I turned back to Linda. "I am *powerfully* thirsty."

"What can I get you?" she asked. "I have the other vial."

I cringed. "I'm a vampire, not a cannibal." Taking my new and improved senses for a test drive, I sniffed in a disturbing aroma. "What's that smell?" My attention turned to the source, Barbie.

Barbie looked at her hands. "My bad. I was chopping garlic for your soup."

"Damn," I said. "I'm going to miss garlic."

"What about your red wine there?" Barbie said. "You love that."

"Red wine is so 1946," I said.

"What will you drink instead?" Barbie asked.

I smiled at Polly. "Once my teeth come in later this evening, I'll think of something."

December 18, 1974—Woodlawn Cemetery, the Bronx, New York City

The night had turned even colder, and the man's skin showed signs of the stress. I would have to feed soon, or the taste would be less satisfying.

"So," I continued, "in order to stay in seclusion at my true love, my mansion, I pretended to move to Beverly Hills, where I staged my death a few years later. Linda helped me with that; then she passed on a few years after that. I never did turn her, much to her chagrin. But creating another vampire is an intensely personal commitment, and I wasn't ready to make it."

I took a deep breath. "Now Barbie keeps me company. I'm grateful she forgave me for drinking her mother and chose to stay with me. She's asked me to turn her before she dies, so we can stay together."

I looked at the gravesite of my only bride. "That's why I came, Milly. To ask your permission. I stayed away, like you asked, and let you live your life. I know I failed you as a husband. My public affair with Marion Davies must have been so painful, and embarrassing, for you. I'm sorry."

A stiff wind rammed against my back. "Now I'm begging for your permission to wed again. To take Barbie as my eternal bride."

I heard Milly's voice in the wind. I had my answer.

Forgiving to the end, my Milly.

2017—Hearst Castle, San Simeon, California

Barbie and I watch from the dark shadows of Casa Grande as the day's final tour departs. I never get tired of the view from my "Enchanted Hill." Barbie, the only woman I've ever turned, squeezes my hand, much like seventy years ago.

"Want to have some fun tonight?" she asks.

That can mean only one thing. My young bride wants to scare the locals.

"I don't know," I reply. Even vampires get tired, and I'm much older than she is.

"Come on. It'll be fun. The legend that this place is haunted is part of its charm."

She's right about that. Ghost hunters rival art aficionados when it comes to tourist visits each day. Imagine if the guests knew what was inside two of the coffins in our collection. Now, that would be a story.

And once in a while, we give them what they want. A show after the sun sets, to keep the legend thriving.

People are so gullible. I mean, seriously, who believes in ghosts?

Magdalena

Lani Forbes

Mission San Juan Capistrano
December 1812

The empty mud nests of the swallows sat nestled into the sandstone archways of the Great Stone Church. The birds had already left for their annual migration, but they had not wasted any time adding their own touches to the architectural wonder that was the new basilica. Magdalena Ruiz still could not believe the church was finally finished. She had been only one year old when construction began, and now, fifteen years later, they finally had a chapel big enough to accommodate the natives and the Spanish families that called the mission home. Though the walls were still bare, they would not be for long.

"Why do you have to paint the plaster when it's wet?" Magdalena pressed her fingertips into the sticky white paste Teofilo had just spread across the stone with a rusty metal trowel.

"The pigment of the paint"—Teofilo's voice sounded slightly muffled from the paintbrush clenched between his teeth—"is absorbed by the wet plaster. When it dries, the paint becomes a part of the wall instead of just covering over it."

"So that you can't chip it away." Magdalena tilted her head thoughtfully as she considered the blank canvas before them.

"No, *mi querida*, the wall and the paint become inseparable. Nothing can take them apart."

Magdalena's pulse quickened at the intensity burning behind his dark eyes as he turned to give her a crooked smile.

She chirped a laugh in response. "Don't let me distract you, I know you only have until it dries to finish the painting."

Teofilo growled a deep sound inside his throat. "You are a distraction simply by being yourself." He quirked a playful eyebrow.

Magdalena was sure the blush blooming across her cheeks was a deeper red than the sinopia pigment crusting along the edges of his clay bowl. "But don't worry. I will finish in time to meet you in the gardens later."

Magdalena didn't doubt Teofilo would finish his painting in time. He was the most talented young artist in all of Alta California.

"How do you make the eyes so realistic?"

Teofilo sighed, though good-naturedly.

"I carve into the plaster as well as paint. It gives depth and dimension, especially to the eyes."

"It's beautiful." Magdalena balanced an elbow on the hard wooden armrest of the pew and rested her chin against her hand.

"Not as beautiful as you, *querida*."

A throat cleared behind them just as the bells of the massive tower above them clanged with such deafening volume that the stones themselves seemed to vibrate with the sound.

Magdalena's arm slipped off the armrest as she spun to find her father framed in the wooden doorway. The golden buttons of a

Spanish military uniform glinted in the light of the burning candles, and the tails of his dark blue coat buffeted slightly in the hot, dry wind blowing in through the open doors. As impressive as he always looked, he looked far from impressed to find his daughter alone in the company of a lowly artist.

Teofilo leaped off the floor as though the stone tiles had turned to lit coals. He inclined his head and kept his chin against his chest in respect.

Her father's nostrils flared slightly as he crossed his arms over his barrel chest. "Magdalena, you are supposed to be in the kitchens helping with dinner."

"I am so sorry, sir. I will head there straightaway." She swore she saw her father give Teofilo a glare sharper than a bayonet before the older man followed her out into the courtyard.

"Magdalena," he said once they were out of earshot of the Great Stone Church. "I do not want you associating with a boy like him."

Magdalena came to a halt and whirled to face her father. "A boy like him? Father, Teofilo is one of the most famous artists in all of—"

"Exactly!" he thundered. "He is an artist! He is not a soldier, not a trader. He owns no lands or property. There is no way a boy like that would ever be able to provide for you or a family. I forbid you from seeing him again."

Tears pricked behind her eyes as she balled her hands into fists. "But I love him, Father."

"You are sixteen. You do not even know what love is, my dear. You will marry a wealthy landowner who will actually be able to take care of you. You are beautiful. I am sure many wealthy suitors will fall at your feet to—"

"But—"

He raised a hand and Magdalena flinched. She bit back her response and fixed her eyes on the dirt swirling around her feet.

"Yes, sir, as you wish."

"Promise me, Magdalena."

"I promise. I will not see him a-a-again." Her voice cracked, but she held his gaze.

"You are dismissed." He waved a flippant hand, his jaw still clenched tight.

Magdalena turned and bolted toward the barracks that housed the soldiers and their families with tears streaming down her cheeks. Despite what she had promised her father, he could not keep her from seeing Teofilo again. They were paint and plaster. Their hearts had already solidified into one, and nothing her father did could separate them now.

Later that night, after the rhythmic breathing of her father drifted in from his room, Magdalena crawled through her open adobe window. A half-moon hung over her like a giant judgmental eye, casting its light over the trickling fountains and vines snaking across the brick walls and arches of the mission. The embers of a fire still burned between the adobe huts of the natives, so she hugged the shadows along the edge of the building until she reached the alcove.

Warm arms greeted her, followed by warm lips, which caressed her mouth softer than the petals of a golden poppy. Magdalena pressed herself against him, desperate for the feel of the safety and adoration that he alone could provide.

"I'm so sorry, Teo. My father . . ."

"Forget him. We can run away together and—" But she never heard what they would do. At that moment a hand wrapped itself around the thick dark braid hanging down her back and yanked her roughly to her feet.

Magdalena cried out in pain, and Teofilo leaped to his feet in an instant, a dagger in his hand.

"Put that away, boy, or I will have you hanged."

Magdalena's stomach dropped at her father's voice. He brought her face inches from his own, his teeth bared beneath the coarse black hair of his finely trimmed mustache.

"You promised me, Magdalena. You have dishonored yourself and you have dishonored me." Magdalena arched her back against the pain radiating down from her scalp and she whimpered slightly. Her father released his grip on her hair only to bring his hand down against the side of her face. Pain exploded across her cheek and stars danced in her eyes before she hit the ground.

"You will confess your sins to the priest during the service tomorrow. You will do penance with the proper shame deserving of your betrayal. Then we will find you a husband. I am going to get you as far away from this mission as I can. If Teofilo comes anywhere near you again, I will have the boy killed. Do you understand me?"

Magdalena pushed herself up to her hands and knees, dirt now coating her face, along with a stinging reminder of her disobedience.

"Yes, Father." She couldn't think of anything else to say—any other way to escape his wrath. Magdalena knew her father. He would hunt her down to the ends of the earth if she tried to escape with Teofilo, and—she hated to admit it—Teofilo wouldn't be able to support them even if she did.

She was trapped. A bird within her father's cage. It did not matter that her heart belonged to Teofilo, when her life belonged to her father. Magdalena let out a sob as the reality of her situation hit her harder than her father's hand. She wouldn't be able to see Teofilo again. Ever.

"Get out of here, you worthless wasp." Her father reached for the gun at his belt. Teofilo stood his ground, staring down her father like a stubborn burro.

"Please, Teo. Go." Magdalena rose shakily to her feet. Tears ran tracks through the dirt on her cheeks.

"Lena, I—" The heartbreak in his voice and the sheen in his eyes shattered her heart into dust.

"I can't go with you. I can't be with you anymore. I'm so sorry."

Teofilo glared at her father, hate etched into every exquisite line of his face, before he turned back to Magdalena.

"I will never stop loving you, until the end of my days and beyond."

"Until the end of my days and beyond," she whispered to her feet. Her shoulders caved in defeat.

Her father grabbed her elbow and jerked her toward their home, away from the freedom she had only gotten to taste and would likely never taste again.

The church bells in the jutting stone tower shook the ground with their cacophony. Travelers often said they could see the tower from ten miles away, but Magdalena was sure the bells could be heard from even farther.

In the back of the church, Magdalena held a candle tight against her chest. The dark veil she wore over her face communicated her shame to the rest of the congregation. Forty or so faces would watch her walk of shame up the center aisle with disgust and disdain in their eyes. Her father waited near the priest at the head of the cathedral, his face grave. Despite the opulence of the Greco-Roman architecture that made it one of the most famous buildings in all of Alta California, Magdalena felt that arches were bars of a cage curving over her head.

Shame burned a hole in her stomach, along with a sick feeling inside her soul that she would never be free—free from her father or from a husband of his choosing. Her heart shed its last bit of hope like a dead leaf as Magdalena took her first step down the aisle.

Where was Teofilo now? Another step.

Would he truly love her until the end of her days? Another step.

Voices hissed and buzzed around her like angry bees, but she kept her eyes on the floor. She did not need to see their judgment when she could feel the weight of it crushing her shoulders. Why had her father insisted on shaming her publicly in front of so many?

Another step.

A boom like a cannon suddenly shook the church far more effectively than the chiming bells in the tower. The world seemed to vibrate and shake like the tail of a rattlesnake.

Magdalena froze, lifting her eyes to look around at the wide-eyed faces of the congregation. The floor beneath her shifted, lifting and rolling as though the massive rattlesnake was now writhing beneath the stones.

That's when the screaming started. Magdalena knew that Alta California frequently rocked with tremors from deep within the earth, but she had never experienced anything like this in her life. The shaking never seemed to end.

Bodies pushed past her, streaming for the door like ants fleeing from the rain. But when they reached the wooden doors of the Great Stone Church, the doors would not open. One look at the now slanting doorframe told her that they would not be able to get out. They were all trapped within the cathedral.

The floor continued to roll beneath her, and she gripped the candle tightly in her palm as though holding on to something could give her stability as the world around her shifted.

A loud cracking sound drowned out the sounds of the screaming. Magdalena only had time to marvel at the sight of the arches, the bars to her cage, crumbling before the stones of the bell tower collapsed onto the roof of the Great Stone Church.

Her last thought was of Teofilo, of the feel of his lips and his hands on her own. She realized she would escape her father's plan for her life after all, and Magdalena smiled as the cathedral collapsed on top of her.

Teofilo ran toward the cloud of dust now obscuring where the Great Stone Church once stood. He screamed her name, but he knew it would be no use. He raced onto the rubble, ignoring the stains of blood coating the stones as he wrenched bricks aside—one after another after another. He had to find her. He had to save her.

Other members of the mission community ran to assist, but after hours of digging, after more rumblings from the earth locking the debris in even tighter around its captives, even Teofilo admitted the futility of finding any survivors. Finally, Teofilo shifted one last stone, and beneath it, a broken, bloodstained candle lay curled in a small tanned hand.

A penitent candle.

Something tight squeezed around his chest, and he wailed as he grasped her cold hand.

He kissed the fingers and uncurled them. Teofilo clutched the candle tightly, swearing to the heavens that he would never forget her. He hated himself for not having done more to try to save Magdalena from her overbearing father. He should have fought for her. He should have whisked her far away from this place.

Until the end of their days and beyond. He'd promised he would love her until the end of her days. He'd had no idea how soon his promise would come true. Teofilo vowed that the next fresco he painted would be of a beautiful dark-eyed angel with flowing hair the color of cacao and a curious glint in her eye.

Spanish officials left the ruins as a cemetery in remembrance of those who lost their lives during the earthquake that destroyed the

Great Stone Church at Mission San Juan Capistrano. Scientists estimate the quake registered magnitude 6.9. To this day, on the night of a half-moon, legend says that visitors to the mission can see the face of a young woman illuminated by the light of a candle in the remaining windows of the ruined church—Magdalena still doing penance for her forbidden love.

Solving for X

Anne Moose

Daniel would be arriving any moment, and Sandra was nervous. Was it a "date"? She wasn't sure. She'd been Daniel's math tutor over the last semester, and he'd called that morning and asked if he could take her out to celebrate his A in algebra. He'd needed a B to qualify for a university football scholarship, and with her help, he'd gotten one of the best grades in the class, had killed on the final. He'd said on the phone that he owed his scholarship, his future, to her—that she was his "favorite person in the world."

Favorite person in the world. Sandra couldn't stop repeating the phrase in her head. She had spent four to five hours a week with Daniel over the last few months, and when she wasn't with him, he was all she could think about. It was torture waiting until the next time she would see him. Sometimes she'd think up excuses to call him. "How about tomorrow we meet at two thirty instead of three o'clock?" she'd suggest. She'd change the time simply to exchange a few words with him, to hear his voice on the phone.

They normally met at three o'clock on Mondays and Wednesdays in the cafeteria of their junior college. Most times they met for two hours, but sometimes, when they got to talking, their meetings went longer. Sandra could tell by the way Daniel sometimes looked at her that he found her attractive. She'd caught him looking at her legs a few times, and being "busted" had made him flash the smile that was his most perfect feature.

She thought practically everything about him was perfect, from the sound of his laugh to the scent of his skin. She loved his scent when he leaned in close to study a problem. Just thinking about it made her crazy. But the thing that made her the craziest was not knowing how he felt about her. When they were together, it seemed as if magic were *trying* to happen, but something, some unseen force, kept it at bay. Maybe Daniel was just being sensible. What would be the point of starting something with her when he'd be leaving California soon for summer football training and then starting a new school in the fall? Sandra knew it might also be that she was white and Daniel was black. Interracial couples were not common in 1970, especially in a town like Fresno. Maybe Daniel dismissed her as a candidate for a girlfriend or thought she dismissed him. She'd tried in every way possible to let him know that she was not that type of person, but she'd never had the courage to address the subject directly.

Tonight, on what she prayed was a real date, she vowed to finally bring it up. It's true that he was leaving in just a couple of weeks, and it was going to break her heart to see him go, but she didn't care. She needed to know how he felt.

When the knock on her door finally came, Sandra's heart began to race. Taking a deep breath, she opened the door, and there he was, with his glorious movie-star smile, holding a bouquet of flowers. A moment later he was in her living room, and suddenly all the chemistry between them was so obvious, so strong, that no words were even necessary. Within ten seconds they were kissing, and Sandra wondered how she could ever have doubted that it would happen.

When they finally paused to smile at one another, Daniel was the first to speak. "You know I'll be leaving soon," he said. "I've been telling myself for weeks that this is a bad idea, but I just couldn't take it anymore."

Sandra laughed nervously and shook her head. "I've been such a wreck—thinking about you, wanting this to happen."

Daniel smoothed back a loose strand of her hair, then hugged her tight.

Sandra could tell by the force of his embrace that he had deep feelings. When he finally let her go, he whispered, "What are you thinking?"

Sandra was filled up with love. "I'm thinking if we only have a few days, I'll take a few days."

With that, they resumed kissing, unleashing a passion that lasted exactly two weeks.

The weeks and months following Daniel's departure were unbearable. Though she knew it was going to kill her, Sandra had agreed not to pursue a long-distance relationship—to make a clean break. Daniel had assured her that he cared for her, maybe even loved her, but said that trying to maintain a relationship from so far away would be too hard, too frustrating.

Despite her feelings, Sandra knew it made sense. They couldn't afford long-distance phone calls, let alone airfare between California and Michigan. They'd even agreed not to write, the theory being that writing would make their separation more difficult. Sandra knew that no matter what, it was going to be difficult. And it was. It was more painful than she could ever have imagined. And the pain lasted a good long time.

Sandra had rushed to set things up for the morning. She still had a hard time believing that there were people interested in wine tasting so early in the day, but she'd had people coming in early all week. Sandra was a graduate student at the University of San Francisco, on break between semesters, and she had agreed to fill in at the winery for her sister Rachel, who was off on a bike tour with her husband, who was part owner of the winery. The job was easy enough. She simply poured wine for tourists and spouted lingo from a script Rachel had given her, dutifully using terms like "fruity" and "full-bodied."

As it turned out, it was not such a busy morning. She'd had two young couples meander in around ten o'clock and then nothing for the next hour, so she'd been lazily reading a book, enjoying the smell of cut grass blowing in through the open window. She loved Napa Valley, with its rolling hills and blue skies, and she marveled at the relative stability of her sister's life.

Around noon, Sandra heard the jingle of the bell on the screen door and looked up to see a couple in their fifties heading for the tasting bar. She greeted them, told them to "have a seat," and then put a glass and short menu in front of each of them.

"What do you think?" she asked after a few minutes. They were staring blankly at the pages in front of them. "Would you like to start with something light?"

The woman looked weary. The man patted her hand. "We don't have to do this if you're not up to it," he said. "The kids meant well, but this is probably not our thing. Maybe we can just take a nice walk. Get some fresh air."

"There's no pressure," Sandra said. They reminded her of Ossie Davis and Ruby Dee. "If you don't feel like tasting today, that's fine. We have beautiful grounds if you want to take a walk around. I can even arrange a tour."

The woman sighed. "You're very sweet." Then she added with a confidential air, "This weekend is a gift from my daughter and son-in-law, but I'm just not sure we're ready."

Her husband pulled out a handkerchief and blew his nose. "We lost our son a couple of months ago," he said. "They're trying to cheer us up. You know, get us out of the house." He stuffed the cloth back into his pocket. "We're staying in a hotel just up the road a ways. We drove up yesterday from Fresno."

Now the woman looked like she might cry, and Sandra was unsure what to do. She grabbed a basket of muffins from behind the counter. "I grew up in Fresno," she said, placing the muffins in front of the couple.

The woman's face brightened. "No kidding. You're a Fresno gal?"

"Sure am," Sandra said. Then she added, "I'm sorry. I should have introduced myself. I'm Sandra."

"You're not Sandra English, are you?" the man asked.

"Don't be ridiculous, Frank," the woman said. But the look on Sandra's face made her think again. "You're not Sandra English."

"That would be me," Sandra said, startled by the strange turn of the conversation. She looked at the gentleman with a quizzical smile.

"Lord have mercy," the woman said.

The man looked at his wife in astonishment. "You can say that again." He turned to Sandra. "Did you go to Fresno Community College?" When Sandra nodded, he added, "I think I'll have that drink now."

Sandra poured the man a glass of wine, then set the bottle down and looked at the couple expectantly.

The woman started to say something, then stopped and turned to her husband for help.

"In our house, you were known as 'the fair princess,'" he said.

The woman gave her husband a disapproving look. "Oh, for Pete's sake, Frank." She turned back to Sandra. "Do you remember a young man named Daniel Sutton?"

Sandra suddenly understood who was sitting in front of her, and her face heated up.

The bell on the door tinkled, and a middle-aged couple walked in. "I'm sorry," Sandra called to them, "but this is a private tasting. You'll have to come back later."

When the intruders were gone, the woman continued. "You remember Daniel?"

"Oh yes," Sandra replied. She felt a familiar pain at hearing his name spoken. "I'll never forget Daniel. It broke my heart when he left for Michigan and I never heard from him again."

"Well, it was rough on him, too," the woman said. "He talked about you incessantly before he went off. It was his brother and sister who called you 'the fair princess.' They teased Daniel a lot. You know how siblings can be." She frowned. "All that business about not having a long-distance relationship, not writing, that was Frank's fault." She looked sideways at her husband. "You should have stayed out of it."

"I have to confess," the man said, "I was not happy about Daniel pursuing a white girl. I felt he was asking for trouble. But he was gone on you, all right. Now, looking back, I probably should have left it alone."

The woman pursed her lips. "I'm going to tell her, Frank." Sandra's sense of alarm was growing by the second. "What do you mean? Tell me what?"

"Oh, darling," said the woman, "sweet Daniel got hurt the second week of practice. Some big brute hit him hard and broke his back."

Sandra was suddenly flooded with memories of unanswered letters, nights spent crying, and months of regret. "So you're saying he came back after just a few weeks and didn't want to tell me?"

"Well, he was in the hospital for a good long while," Daniel's mother explained. "He was in for at least a couple of months, wasn't he, Frank?"

Her husband nodded.

"We encouraged him to contact you," she continued, "but Daniel was stubborn. It was clear, early on, that he was headed for a wheelchair, and he just insisted that you not be told. He was afraid of 'being a burden' and all that type of nonsense. I told him it should be your decision."

Sandra found the woman's words almost too painful to process. "I did actually write to him," she said. "Do you know if he ever got my letters?"

Her question was met with silence as the couple looked at each other. Finally, the woman spoke up. "The university did forward some letters, and I'm ashamed to say we kept them from Daniel."

"He was already so broken up," the man said. "And he was clear about not wanting to involve you." He frowned. "We thought the letters might make things worse."

Sandra's head was swimming with so many mixed emotions that she was unable to think straight.

"In those early days, it was a struggle just to convince him to want to live," the woman explained. "He took the accident very hard. Remember, he was an athlete. It was a lot for him to accept. In the beginning, especially, things were very tough." She searched Sandra's face for understanding. "We felt you might be able to help, but Daniel was adamant, so we went along."

"Did anyone read my letters?" Sandra asked.

The couple exchanged a look, then shook their heads in unison. "I don't recall what we did with the letters," the woman said, "but I'm certain that no one ever opened them. That would have been wrong."

Sandra took a deep breath and struggled not to cry. After years of pain and uncertainty, she suddenly understood why she'd never heard from Daniel again.

The woman opened her purse and pulled a laminated photograph out of her wallet. She handed it to Sandra. "Here's Daniel at his graduation from Berkeley," she said. "He got a degree in electrical engineering." Her lips quivered. "That was probably the proudest day of my life."

Looking at the picture, Sandra was immediately struck by the smile that had so won her heart. "He looks exactly like I remember him," she said, her voice cracking with emotion. She tried to control herself, but despite her best efforts, she began to tremble, and then cry.

The couple looked at each other, and then suddenly the man cried, "Oh my goodness! You must be thinking that it was Daniel who died. But, no, it was his older brother Markus we lost. He was in a car accident up near Lake Tahoe."

"Oh, Lord!" his wife exclaimed. "I don't know how we could have been so thick. Sweetheart, Daniel is fine." She took Sandra's hand. *"He's fine."* She looked at her husband, then back at Sandra, who was struggling with so many feelings that she was dizzy.

"I don't know how you feel about this," the woman continued, "but I think we need to tell Daniel that we've seen you." She turned to her husband for his reaction.

He nodded, then looked down at Sandra's hand, which was still in his wife's grip. "You aren't wearing a wedding ring."

Sandra began deep breathing in an effort to calm herself. "I'm single," she said. "And I would love to see Daniel, if he'll agree to it."

Daniel had mixed feelings as he awaited Sandra's arrival. He was eager to see her, but he tried not to let his hopes soar too high. He'd had a couple of short relationships over the last two years, but each time his disabilities had proven too much for the woman to handle. And neither had compared favorably to Sandra, whom he'd never stopped thinking about during the four years since his injury. He'd wondered endlessly what her life was like and had been tempted many times to contact her. It seemed now that fate had intervened. Even their proximity seemed fated. She lived in San Francisco, and he in Oakland. He wanted so much to reconnect with her, and for things between them to work out, but he was terrified that she'd simply stir up his feelings and then leave him like the others had done. She'd sounded positive on the phone, but also mysterious, claiming there were things she wanted to tell him face-to-face.

Daniel was in the process of regretting, for the umpteenth time, that he couldn't greet her standing up, when the knock on the door came and sent his adrenaline racing. He took a deep breath, rolled his chair across the hardwood floor, and pulled open the door.

It took him several seconds to process the vision that met him at his doorstep.

"Can we come in?" Sandra asked. She was glowing in a blue and yellow sundress, and looked even better than Daniel remembered.

"Please," he managed with a nervous laugh. His mind was spinning and his heart pounded in his chest.

He rolled his chair backward to make way, his eyes fixed on the beautiful brown boy in her arms.

"This is Xavier," Sandra announced. "X for short." She turned to the little boy, whose dark eyes were shining. "Xavier, this is Daniel."

She placed the little boy on the floor, and Daniel stared at him, transfixed.

"I'm pleased to meet you, Xavier," he said finally, reaching out to shake the boy's tiny hand. He looked up at Sandra and then turned back to the boy, who was wearing overalls and a Superman T-shirt. "How old are you, Xavier?"

The little boy grinned and said, with obvious pride, "Free and a half."

Sandra crouched down and gave her son a kiss on the cheek. Then she lifted him into his father's lap. "This okay?"

The child nodded.

Daniel smiled his perfect smile.

Sandra stepped behind Daniel and folded her arms around his neck.

"You smell good," she whispered.

Splash

D. P. Lyle

It was the voices that first attracted her attention, disembodied murmurings that seemed to flow from the dense fog. At first she thought they came from her imagination, maybe from the waves that lapped against her kayak, perhaps distant whale songs. But no, she decided, they were real.

It was nearing 10:00 p.m. Sophia Gonzalez had been on the water for two hours, doing her usual laps off the Newport coast. She did twenty miles on most nights. Tonight maybe more, prepping for her August trip to the San Juan Islands to see the orcas up close, eye level.

When she'd left the harbor just after sunset, the sky had been clear, filled with stars and a low three-quarter moon, but this was June, and soon the fog had rolled in, thick, cool, damp. Her skin was slick, her hair hanging in strings, wet from sweat and the dense air. Her GPS watch had her on course to return to Newport Harbor, now only two miles away. She slowed to a glide, laying her double paddle across her thighs, wiping the moisture from her face with a small towel. That's when the voices materialized.

At first they were unclear, broken, buried in the thick air and the waves tapping against her hull. She was able to grab the words only in bits and pieces. Probably fishermen. She considered calling out, letting them know she was nearby, to maybe avoid a collision, but something about them made her hesitate.

"What . . . boss?" A male voice.

"Throw . . . overboard." Also male but with a raspy quality.

"No . . . Please." A third male, high-pitched, laced with fear.

Her breath caught. She gripped the paddle as the kayak lifted and settled with each ocean swell.

"Tell . . . where . . ."

"I . . . my brother."

She searched the gray soup but saw nothing. They seemed close, but she knew that in fog sounds carried far and wide, making distances deceiving. Could be twenty feet or a hundred yards. She sensed they were to her right, to the south, but determining direction was also a problem in air this thick.

"Then you'll pay the price."

"Please." A plaintive keening.

The voices were now much clearer. She must be drifting toward them. What to do? Sit tight, hope she remained invisible? Paddle away? If so, in which direction?

"I'll find him anyway." The raspy voice. "You know that."

"It wasn't him."

She dipped a paddle into the water but couldn't bring herself to stroke. Would they hear the churned water?

"We both know that's not true."

Something *clunk*ed in the darkness. A metallic sound. Chains dropping against a hard surface?

"Tell me where he is." The raspy voice now carried a menacing urgency. "And where my fucking money is."

"I don't know. I swear."

"Toss him."

Now she heard the unmistakable clatter of chains.

"Please don't do this."

More rattling, pleading, begging, and then a gasp and a hard splash. She jerked to attention. Only ten seconds passed before the splash wave rocked her kayak. She was close. Too close.

"That should take care of Mr. Jimmy Dolans," the raspy voice said. "Now let's find his fucking brother."

A fullness rose in her chest. She had to move. Now. She glanced at the illuminated dial of her watch, reoriented herself toward shore, and carefully dipped one blade into the water. Slow even strokes, right, left, praying the swish of each was soft enough not to give her away.

Then it happened.

One sweat-slicked hand slipped from the paddle, which banged against the hull of her kayak with a sharp *crack*.

"What was that?" The younger voice.

"What's what?" The raspy voice.

"I heard something. Over there."

A smear of light appeared to her right. A flashlight, scouring the water. It was maybe a hundred feet away. She held the paddle tightly against her chest, her breathing halted. She resisted the urge to slash at the water, to race away from them. No way they could see her. For them, the fog would only scatter the light, creating a white, frosted-glass screen. But if she panicked and fled, they would hear and would know for sure she was there. And where.

"Turn off that fucking light," the raspy voice said. "You trying to blind me?"

It winked off. Everything was now dark, still.

"What'd you hear?"

"Sounded like a clunk. Like a plank dropping on a floor. Something like that. Maybe a boat striking a log or a piece of wood."

"Out here? Middle of nowhere? In this shit?"

"I'm just saying it's what I heard."

"Jesus. Let's get out of here."

A brief silence and then a motor churned to life. The engine thrummed the water, but thankfully began to recede. To the south. She waited until it faded, then clambered toward shore.

"You sure you heard what you heard?"

Sophia sat across the desk from her boss, Wally Spencer, editor of *SPLASH* magazine, a glossy local publication that dealt with all things Newport Beach. If you needed the scoop on an OC event or a new restaurant, or maybe a piece on a local bigwig, *SPLASH* had it. Sophia handled most of the "society" interviews.

"No, I'm not sure. I stayed up half the night trying to make sense of it." She ran through her story again. "What does it sound like to you?"

Wally lifted his glasses and pinched the bridge of his nose, which he always did when he was troubled by something. "I don't know what to think."

"If you ask me, someone got wrapped in chains and tossed in the ocean."

He sighed. "Anyone named Dolans missing?"

"I checked with my guy at the Newport Beach PD. Nothing."

Wally nodded.

"But maybe he hasn't been reported missing yet," Sophia said. "It's only been a few hours."

"Is that Dolans with an *s* or with a *z*?"

"Wally, they didn't skywrite it. And the transmission, so to speak, was a bit fuzzy."

He smiled.

"I'll check the phone book. Make some calls," she said.

He nodded. "Let me know."

She walked back to her office. Mason Turley, *SPLASH*'s main photographer and her close friend, was bent over her desk, scribbling something on a yellow sticky note.

"Mason?"

He looked up. "Just leaving you a message." He picked up the speargun he had leaned against her chair. "Look what I got you."

"I have one."

"Yeah, but it's a piece of crap. This one's brand-new. State-of-the-art."

She took it from him and examined it. "You shouldn't have. Mine is just fine."

"No, it's not. Besides, I can't have someone with defective equipment fishing with me."

"Thanks," she said. "We still diving tomorrow morning?"

"Yep. I'll pick you up at six."

He left and she sat at her desk. She lifted her phone book from the upper right drawer, flipped it open, and quickly found three Dolanses and two Dolenzes. None were Jimmy or James. She started with the Dolanses. The first two were a bust—no answer and a woman who thought she was selling subscriptions to the magazine and told her off before hanging up. The third was a different story.

"Is this the residence of Jimmy Dolans?" Sophia asked. She could hear a TV in the background. Sounded like a game show.

"It is," the woman said.

"Can I speak with him?"

"If he were here. But he isn't."

"Do you know when he'll be back?"

"No. And I don't know where he is. But I'd like to."

"Oh?"

"He went out last night. Haven't heard from him since."

Sophia felt her heart skip a beat, then drop into her stomach. "Are you related to him?"

"I'm Adele Dolans. His mother. Who are you?"

"I'm Sophia Gonzalez. With *SPLASH* magazine."

"Why would you be looking for Jimmy? What's he done now?"

"Nothing that I know. It's just a story I'm working on."

"And this story involves Jimmy?" She snorted. "What's it about?"

She hadn't expected that question and searched for an answer. Better to avoid it, she decided. "I'd better talk to Jimmy about it."

"That sounds like some kind of trouble. Again. Are the police involved this time?"

"The police? Why would you think that?"

"Wouldn't be the first time. Those boys'll be the death of me."

"Boys?"

"Yeah. Jimmy and his brother."

Brother? Her heart descended another step. "Is his brother around?"

"Tommy? No. He took off for Colorado three days ago. All of a sudden. Said he had some business to take care of. Now, I ask you, what kind of business would a seventeen-year-old have in Colorado?"

"Mrs. Dolans, can I drop by and talk with you?"

"About what? Jimmy and Tommy?"

"Yes."

"You still haven't told me why."

"I think we should chat face to face."

She sighed. "I was just heading out to a doctor's appointment. How about in a couple of hours?"

"That'll work."

The address Adele Dolans gave was in upper Newport, just off Sixteenth Street and Dover Avenue in Newport's Back Bay. A wealthy neighborhood, as were all enclaves in Newport Beach. The house was a neat ranch style, the yard well manicured, the trees expertly trimmed.

The front door stood ajar.

Sophia rapped on the frame. "Mrs. Dolans?"

No response. She repeated the call and again got nothing back. She nudged the door open farther and looked into the living room. Also neat. Well furnished. Quiet. No TV game show going now. She stepped inside.

"Mrs. Dolans?"

Her voice echoed in the empty room. She took a few steps, then froze. To her right, an archway led into a dining room. A woman slumped in a chair, only the ropes that bound her preventing her from sliding to the floor. Her head lolled to one side, her face a bloody mess, nose flattened, one eye purple and swollen closed, the other black and lifeless. A red blossom smeared the front of her white blouse.

Sophia's head swiveled. Was the killer still here? Watching her?

She raced out the door to her car. Inside, she punched the lock button and called 911 and then Detective Sean Archer, her friend at the Newport Beach PD. Ten minutes later a police cruiser, lights flashing, rolled into the drive. Two uniformed officers jumped out, guns unholstered. Sean's car chirped against the curb behind her car. He stepped out, raising a finger, indicating she should sit tight.

Sean, his gun hanging loosely in his right hand, and the officers approached the front door.

Sophia climbed from her car and watched the trio enter the home. She half expected to hear gunshots. The minutes dripped by until Sean came out and headed her way.

"You okay?" he asked.

"No."

"How'd you walk into this?"

She told him the story. He raised an eyebrow more than once, started to interrupt a couple of times, but she waved him away. She needed to get it out all at once. When she fell silent, he spoke.

"Let me get this straight. You heard some guys throw someone in the ocean. Heard the name 'Jimmy Dolans,' called the mother, and came by to talk with her. Is that about it?"

His face blurred through the tears gathering in her eyes. "She said Jimmy didn't come home last night. Said his brother, Tommy, took off all of a sudden. Three days ago. To Colorado, according to what he told her."

He nodded.

"What is it?" she asked. "You know something."

"And you're a good reporter."

"Meaning?"

"Jimmy and Tommy are on our radar. Low-level drug dealers. We've been building a connection to their supplier."

"Who is?"

"This is off the record. Okay?"

"I don't do crime stories."

"You should. You'd be great at it. But you can't start with this. Okay?"

She nodded.

"The Dolans brothers are hooked up with guy named Jack Watson. He's plugged in to the Sinaloa supply lines. Runs meth, marijuana, oxy, you name it, up through Tijuana."

"And the other guy? On the boat? I heard two distinct voices."

"I'd bet on Jose Garcia. One of Watson's crew."

"No offense, but if you know who they are and what they do, why are these guys walking around free?"

"No offense taken." He smiled. "They're out and about so we can track them. Maybe get higher up the food chain. Find the guy from the cartel who's supplying them." He shrugged. "It's how the game's played."

She shook her head. "Didn't look like a game to me." She nodded toward the house.

"Sorry you saw that," he said.

"Me too."

"Maybe I can make it up to you."

"Let me guess. Dinner?"

He shrugged. "I've only asked a dozen times, and every time you've said no."

"Eleven. You've asked me eleven times now." She smiled. "But who's counting?" She laid a hand on his arm. "What if I say yes?"

"We have dinner. At the place of your choice." He smiled. "Simple, huh?"

"On one condition."

"Name it."

"Pick me up. I need to drink. A lot. Too much to be driving."

He laughed. "Deal."

"Eight o'clock?"

"I'll be there. Eight o'clock sharp."

She smiled. "I love punctuality."

"That's me. Punctual to a fault."

Sophia was nervous about her date with Sean. She wasn't sure why. She'd always found him attractive and had been tempted each time he'd asked her out. But he was a source. A business contact.

He'd given her a heads-up on several Newport Beach scandals and other shenanigans. Each made for good copy. Better interviews. Was this mixing pleasure with business? Sure. But after today, after what she'd seen, life seemed decidedly less predictable. Maybe a night out with a hot guy was a good thing. Lord knew it'd been months since she'd had a real date.

She was ready early. She had opted for gray slacks and a dark blue silk shirt. Eventually. After trying on three different outfits. So unlike her. She usually grabbed the first thing she saw in her closet. Why did Sean make her anxious? So girly? She hated that feeling. His smile. That was it. The way it lit up his face and deepened those little crow's-feet at the corners of his eyes. His sexy blue eyes.

She still had twenty minutes before he arrived, so she worked on the speargun Mason had given her. She wiped it down, snapped a spear into position along the barrel, and then tested the two rubber bands. New and stiff. She stretched them a few times before placing the speargun's butt against her chest and tugging one band and then the other into position. She aimed it at the wall. She liked the balance. Seemed very solid. She did wonder how easy it would be early tomorrow morning with the hangover she was sure to have.

Her doorbell buzzed. She glanced at her watch. Ten minutes early. Eager or just overly punctual? With eleven attempts to get her to say yes, she'd bet on the former.

She leaned the speargun against the wall next to her dresser before crossing her living room and opening the front door.

It wasn't Sean. It was two men. One older, the other younger, Hispanic. Each wore jeans, a black T-shirt, and an unfriendly expression.

"Can I help you?"

The younger one spoke. "You Sophia Gonzalez? With *SPLASH* magazine?"

She took a half step back. "Yes. Who are you?"

"A couple of guys who want to know what your story is."

"What? That makes no sense."

She glanced past them, toward the street, hoping to see Sean pull up. "Look, I don't know who you are or what you want, but I'm going to ask you to leave."

"Maybe I can explain things." It was the older guy. His voice was harsh, raspy.

She recognized it immediately. Her breath caught and then expanded like an overinflated balloon, as if trying to push her racing heart through her chest. She suddenly felt cold.

A gun appeared. He flattened his free hand against her chest and shoved her inside. She staggered, nearly falling. The men followed.

"What are you—?"

The older man raised his gun, silencing her. "What'd you tell the cops?"

How did they know?

"It was you," he continued. "On the water last night."

"What?"

"Don't play dumb. I know you were there. I know you heard. I know you've talked to the police. I know you talked with Mrs. Dolans before her unfortunate accident."

"I don't know what you're talking about," Sophia said.

"Just like Mrs. Dolans, you will tell us what you know. Eventually." His eyes narrowed. "And what you shared with the police. Do that and you just might live. If not, we'll splatter your brains all over your lovely apartment." He smiled. "Does that make things clearer?"

"Please."

"Look, Ms. Gonzalez, you're running out of time here. Tell me." He leaned forward, his breath hot on her face. "Now."

Her mind raced. Her gaze bounced to the front door, hoping to see Sean walk in, then toward the kitchen, where an assortment of knives could be easily reached, and finally in the direction of her bedroom.

He tapped her forehead with a finger. "Look at me."

She did.

"Talk."

She swallowed hard. Her hand came up to her mouth. "I'm going to be sick."

"Jesus, lady."

"I'm serious." She turned and raced toward her bedroom, hand still over her mouth, trying to sell the ploy. She expected to feel a bullet rip through her back. Instead she heard the raspy voice.

"Follow her."

Footsteps closed from behind. She snatched up the speargun and whirled around, raising it. Thank God she had armed it. The younger man came through the door. His eyes widened. He lifted his weapon, but the spear beat him. It released with a snap of the bands and slammed into his throat. His pistol thudded against the carpet. He clutched at the spear, blood flowing between his fingers, his breath ragged and wet. He staggered backward and toppled to the living room floor. His chest convulsed twice, and then he fell silent.

"What the fuck?" Raspy Voice said.

Two gunshots, sharp and angry. She dove behind her bed and frantically dug her heels into the carpet until her back was plastered against the wall. Footsteps approached. She still gripped the speargun, but she had no spear. It was worthless. Like a child, she looked at the gap beneath her bed. Her only thought was to crawl beneath it. Hide. Like that would do any good.

Then he appeared at the foot of the bed. Not the man. Sean, his weapon in his hand.

"Are you okay?" he asked.

She jumped to her feet. "I never thought I'd say this, but I'm happy you brought your gun on our date."

He smiled. "And I'm early."

She hugged him tightly. "I love punctuality."

Steps

Phyllis Blake

Anna stared at the San Francisco return address in the unopened letter in her hands. Silverman, Silverman, and Green, Attorneys at Law. What was that about? Putting it on the table by the door, she shuffled quickly through the rest, discarding a handful of junk circulars. The postcard from Arlene, a printed reminder about the ninetieth birthday celebration of their piano teacher and mentor, Madame Eberlé, remained. It included a handwritten notation in purple ink saying that Madame was counting on seeing her and had asked for Brahms as a special favor.

Anna looked at the still-angry surgical scars on her hand, put the card beside the letter, and returned to the kitchen to finish cleaning up the breakfast dishes.

Madame's famous birthday celebrations, as viewed once on a *60 Minutes* segment, had never been mere parties. Her former students, even the ones who hadn't achieved fame, were expected to play, and they practiced as though for important concerts. For star pupils like Anna, the only excuses for not playing were death or retirement. So they would know, her friends and rivals. Most importantly, Madame would know.

But how could she stay away? This would certainly be the last birthday—at ninety a brain tumor was pretty much the final coda. She pictured herself playing Madame's piano all those years ago, the tiny woman seated on her right, her whole being listening and watching, cataloging each hesitation and misstep. Then the analysis, delivered with obsessive attention to detail, and "this finger, not that, pedal here, not there" kind of advice. Finally would come the discussion of the expressive "arc" of the composition and how Anna wanted the musical energy to flow. At the door, Madame would urge her to eat more, to sleep more, to be kinder to herself.

Anna slammed the dishwasher door shut and jabbed at the start button. Walking briskly downstairs to her studio, she went straight to the piano. She owned two Steinways, the one upstairs in her living room, which gleamed as if new, and this one, battle-scarred from moves and careless housekeepers. She wondered if she should go back upstairs and play the other one, with its slightly easier touch. No. She needed her old friend.

Her surgeon had okayed a little gentle playing at her last visit. That had been two days ago. She carefully folded up the Brahms on the music rack and put it away, determined to be realistic and upbeat. Looking in the Bach drawer, she pulled out the two-part inventions. She'd learned these as a ten-year-old, finding them both easy and addictive. She needed easy.

Beginning with the first one, in C major, she put her hands in position and began to play. The left hand still worked, but it hadn't played for a while, so even that hand was stiff. The right hand knew what to do. It kept trying to put fingers in the right places, but mostly they didn't make it, and the pain was distracting.

Stopping for a moment, she reminded herself to slow way down.

Fingers still weren't getting there. In fact, when she stretched for a note, what felt like a physical barrier inside her hand made her misjudge the distance. She tried to compensate with more arm movement. Bad idea.

She stopped again. Why hadn't she realized that even simple Bach required a full range of fingerings and hand movements? Clearly, this was a bad choice.

What she needed was something more basic to start with—perhaps a piece for beginners—something that stayed in five-finger position and gradually extended the reach, like Bartók's *Mikrokosmos* books, something that went step by step from the beginning, something a novice would play, something—

She closed the lid over the keys. Had she thought she'd be ready to play Bach just a couple of weeks after surgery? A surgery that included repairs for carpal tunnel, trigger finger, arthritis, and the removal of a rather large tumor from the top of her hand?

Really?

After grabbing a sweater and her house key, she was on the way out her front door when she noticed the lawyer's letter still on the table. She tore the envelope.

> Dear Ms. Durrell:
>
> It is with sadness and regret that I inform you that your aunt, Mrs. Stella Gavin, passed away very suddenly. As her attorney, it is also my duty to inform you that you are her primary beneficiary. Please be in contact with me as soon as possible so we may begin the process of settling her estate. It would be my pleasure to represent you in this

matter should you desire that; or, if you prefer, I'll make all pertinent documents available to your own attorney.

Your aunt was a friend as well as a client, and I look forward to hearing from you.

Very truly yours,

Robert J. Silverman, Esq.

She was out of the house, around the corner, and halfway down the hill before thought was possible again. *So I have choices,* she thought. *Even now. If I don't want to obsess over the inability to play, I can torture myself over Stella, my only living relative, who left me on a New York street, alone, when I was sixteen years old. Now forever inaccessible.*

Anna stopped. She squeezed her eyes together behind her sunglasses.

Had she actually thought that someday she and her aunt would sit down together and eat turkey at Thanksgiving?

After so many years of silence, all she'd wanted from Stella was to understand why. She remembered that day, when she'd stood mesmerized by the envelope stuffed with cash, enough to keep her at Juilliard for four years, enough to realize her dream. She'd been so entranced by it, she'd failed to notice the woman who'd raised her disappearing into the fast-moving crowd. And when she did look up, Stella was gone.

Bafflement and years of bad dreams had given no answers. To this day, she half expected Stella to suddenly appear in the audience of one of her concerts. *Hopelessly naive,* her aunt's voice said in her head.

Now she must face what had always been true: Stella was completely and absolutely unknowable. Period.

Arriving at the parking lot at the bottom of the hill and looking down the stairs, she stopped.

Straight ahead, the point thrust itself out into the water like the coastline giving the Pacific the finger, and her eyes plainly told her that every step onto that point was a step marching directly into a body of water.

On either side of the point, the water undulated in that familiar, hypnotic pattern. Whenever she watched waves for any length of time, her sense of rhythm engaged. She'd find herself counting beats between waves and trying to anticipate the next one. She'd never solved the metrics of it, of course, but the watching and the counting fascinated her, like counting the rings on a beautifully marked poisonous snake.

Ever since she'd moved to Southern California nine years ago to make a home overlooking the beach, she'd intended to go down to the water and gradually get over her phobia. But like her meaning to quit smoking or take up yoga, months and years had gone by. Living close to the ocean hadn't provided an antidote, not the way she'd hoped.

This could be the right moment. If she ever needed a diversion, it was now. Panic was pretty much all consuming. If she could get to the end of the point, that would do it. No part of her brain would be available for regret or longing. And if somehow she went over the edge into the water, that would be a solution in itself.

But if she succeeded, even for a few moments, surely she herself would change. If she could go down to the end of the point, look over the edge, and survive it, she could face anything. She'd read about people turning their lives around by diving out of airplanes or walking tightropes between twenty-story buildings. Hell, magical thinking was her specialty.

Her feet simply wouldn't move. If she wanted to go forward, a strategy was necessary. Perhaps she could think the way she had when she'd first seen hundreds of people sitting in rows waiting for her to play. By looking down and concentrating on the keys, she'd convinced herself that her eyes lied. Nobody there, just her and the piano. A fanciful solution, but it had worked. Piece of cake.

She wondered about that knack of lying to herself, and about all the skills she'd acquired through years of performing. What did any of it matter anymore? Now that she couldn't play, was any of it useful?

Deliberately placing each foot with care on each step, not looking to the side, she went down the parking lot stairs. At the bottom, she strode quickly past the yogurt and T-shirt shops and the California Coast Gallery. She clamped her teeth together hard and continued past the restaurant's door at the end, where the wall guarding pedestrians from the rocks below gave way to an iron railing.

Tourists were always walking out to the end, holding the corroded rail, feeling the spray on their faces and taking selfies. A sort of Titanic experience. In a strong sea, the surf broke high and hard against the point, cold water splashed over them, and great squeals of consternation competed with the thunder of crashing waves. But today was a good day. Calm. No tourists. She could do this.

The briny smell and the sea-spray dampness began to seep into her nostrils, her hair, and her clothes. She realized how tightly she was holding on to the railing, that it was beginning to hurt, and that her eyes were closed. She told herself to open them.

Mistake.

The sensation of tumbling headfirst into the swirling water overwhelmed her. She held tighter. Her right hand began to shriek of pain from the cold and the pressure of her grip. Her sense of control began to slip away. She shut her eyes again.

"Are you okay?" a man's voice said behind her.

"Perfectly," she said.

A moment passed. "You don't look okay," he said. "I'm right beside you. If you open your eyes, you'll see me."

She raised her head and turned it toward his voice. She opened her eyes. A nice-looking man with a helmet of short, thick, silvery hair and deep-gray eyes was looking at her.

"I'm on a mission," she said.

He nodded. "I can see that."

Tanned, thick, rugged but well groomed, he looked ex-military. Both the US Navy and the Marine Corps had installations nearby. He looked down at the railing.

"Your fingers are turning purple," he said. "Just an observation."

She nodded.

"My hand is right next to yours," he said. "I'll be happy to help if you want to move away from this spot. If your mission allows that."

She nodded. "It's large bodies of water," she said. "Bathtubs are okay."

"Yes," he said. "That makes sense."

"I decided to do something about it. Today."

"Good start," he said. "If you want to, you can take hold of my arm."

She thought about that for a moment. The thinking required was how to let go of the railing and reach toward his arm, not whether she wanted to or not. It was her bad hand, but she thought that if she reached far enough she could lock arms with him. Little by little she did it.

"Good job," he said. He didn't seem to mind that she held his arm clamped in a death grip. "What was your plan? Did you want to go all the way around the point, or back to the parking lot?"

"I don't think I had a plan."

"Then if you don't mind a suggestion, let's go back to the parking lot. Maybe you've been brave enough for one day."

He wasn't quite as tall as she, but he was as formidable as a tank, and he radiated confidence. Putting himself between her and the water, he walked her slowly back toward the stairs. She began to ease up when they were beside the art gallery, and she let go of his arm when they reached the yogurt shop.

"Thank you," she said. "I feel ridiculous."

"Why? You completed your mission. My wife has a similar problem, and she's never gone this far. I congratulate you. If I could offer a bit of advice, though?"

She wasn't quite listening, but she heard his voice go up, so she nodded and tried to pay attention.

"Start small," he said, "with a single step. Go out onto the rocks where it's dry. Every day go a step closer to the water. The tide pools are great. Lots to see. Try that first." He pointed to the south side of the point. "Go during low tide. Anemones, tiny crabs, all kinds of fun, harmless critters. Every day, a step closer."

"Thank you again," she said, holding out her left hand. "My name is Anna."

"Alex," he said, taking it. "Good luck."

She walked up the stairs with him, watched him get into a shiny Lexus sedan, and waved when he drove off. She often saw men like him in restaurants with their wives. He'd hold a chair for his wife, open doors, and go to the car for a forgotten sweater. She supposed the wife would get up at dawn with him, cook breakfast for him, and have dinner ready when he got home. She'd probably never received a standing ovation at the Salzburg Festival, but she had his arm whenever she needed it.

Years ago, in Paris, hand in hand with an outrageously attractive man who was the count of something in old European aristocracy, she'd run laughing through the streets after too much champagne. He'd begged her to go home with him and meet his father. Even at the time it had felt more like a movie than the real thing. She'd treated it all as a game and said goodbye the next morning without a second thought. What would he be like now? Would he have hair? Would his wife serve tea in the drawing room in the afternoons and feed tidbits to the Pekingese beside her on the satin divan?

Would Anna have liked that sort of thing? Would she trade it for playing Brahms?

Later, she sat at the kitchen table with her glass of wine and stared at the Silverman letter. In her head, Stella's voice still laughed at her. Wanting to be a musician was like wanting to be a waiter, she'd said. You could learn to be the very best waiter, and everyone would know your name, but at the end of the day, you were the help. And when you got old and dropped things, they fired you. Catering to overstuffed morons had not been part of Stella's life plan. One day she would sit at the head of the table, she would invite only people who interested her, and she would hire musicians.

Yet it was Stella who'd left the envelope in Anna's hand.

Stella was gone.

As she looked out her dining room window through the tracery of eucalyptus branches, the distant ocean gently sparkled in the moonlight. She sipped her wine and considered her options—either go to Madame's party or walk back to the point and jump off.

After the second glass, she went upstairs and booked the plane and hotel. Then she stood over the paper shredder and fed it the letter from the San Francisco lawyer. Though she'd never found her aunt again, Stella could have made contact herself very easily through Anna's agent, through her recording company, or simply by walking backstage to talk to her after a performance.

Watching the Silverman letter and envelope disappear into the teeth of the shredder was slim satisfaction. It was enough.

Halfway through the third glass she went back upstairs, climbing the steps very carefully this time, holding tightly to the banister. Her fingers successfully logged on to Amazon and ordered the set of *Mikrokosmos*.

The Inevitable Avocado

Jeffrey J. Michaels

I call it the "California Promise." No, not the one of riches and fame, glory and wealth. Rather the one where they say, "Sure, no problem, we'll be there!" and of course something else becomes more important and they make a noble excuse. Or not. Because no one actually expects to receive a reason for the no-show.

Today the band is good enough, and the songs are familiar enough, and the cause is decent enough that it seems not so many people exercised the California Promise of finding someplace else to be this afternoon. The promoter does not care if people do not show. They paid in advance for their tickets. Fewer people mean less time spent dealing with entertainment and crowd satisfaction.

This is a charity event. We have to support the dolphins. Or the whales. Or the surfers. It always seems to come back to surfing in this town. They even trademarked the term "Surf City" and sought to make a profit on merchandise. I think it backfired somehow. Surfers aren't buying a trademarked phrase for their T-shirt line. Or their custom flip-flops. Or their surfboard wax—or whatever, dude.

Warm air wafts around the outdoor patio at the hotel on the beach. One of the big ones, y'know, starts with *H* and struggles hard to maintain a beachcomber image while charging massive prices for a room and a meal.

Of course it is not actually on the beach. Pacific Coast Highway runs between the hotel property and Mother Nature's wide repository of sand. Beyond the well-groomed beach is Mother Ocean. Here the waves are regular and not too large. Grommies and Old Guys Who Rule share the cresting waters with the young guns trying to go pro and catch a wave of sponsorship money. The waves are nice here because of the island, or so I have been told. Just twenty-six miles away according to the song. Some days the island is there and some it is not. Today we can see Catalina clear and close as winds are from the desert.

It is a dry heat. Not like Palm Desert, where it gets so hot your ice melts before you can drink your iced tea—even the famous Starbucks ice, y'know, that can last all day. Here we have the ocean, and no matter how hot the air is as it arrives, Pacific breezes ameliorate the intensity. This morning I stepped from my shower and knew we were having a Santa Ana event when I was dry before I touched my towel.

The buffet is being set and we are listening to the band. Four old guys playing a surf song they wrote fifty years past. Well, only one of them wrote it. Cowrote as it turns out, and there is another band claiming to be the original with the other half of the songwriting duo. They had a fight about copyright and spent more money on lawyers than they ever received from royalties. I am pretty sure they used the law firm that executed the Surf City trademark deal.

I take a picture. That is why I am here. My raison d'être. No one else here would know that phrase.

Of the scheduled celebs only one has shown up—someone famous's son. He has his own radio show, but really, who listens to radio anymore? The guests gather. Fame and fortune. Bump up against it in any form and it might rub off on you. It is all just the illusion of success, but if you can fake it till you make it, other people try to bump up to you.

So the radio-show son-of-a-television-star, who really is pretty nice and fairly witty, gets all the guests' attention until the girl who is famous just for being famous since her nineties youth-oriented cable channel gig arrives and nonchalantly decides to stay when one of her people successfully points her out to a group that is waiting to find someone else who is famous to fawn over without having to wait in line for the radio son. "Hey! Isn't that . . . ?" the assistant says as she stands in a well-lit spot, but out of the too-bright sun. And the crowd squints and says, "Yes. It is her!"

I take a picture of the famous-just-because-she's-famous. I am careful, y'know. Her blond wig is not exactly perfect, her natural dark hair obvious in its escape attempt. I could have snapped a revealing shot that would embarrass her if published. But no one wants to publish that picture of her. It's not like she is a Hollywood big shot waiting to be knocked off her pedestal. She's just a person—trying. Besides, I might make more money from her publicity machine than I would ever make doing the sneak-attack paparazzi thing.

Signaling her attendant, I lean close and say, "I can get some pix for you to use, but you might want to . . ." I point to my own hairline and pretend to be tucking a wisp under an invisible hairpiece. I am blessed with good hair. The ocean responds nicely and ruffles my blond curls. The attendant takes a moment to gather my meaning, smiling weirdly at me as comprehension dawns on him that I am not propositioning him, and then follows my exaggerated nod and gaze to his mistress's plight. She somehow notes my gaze.

Perhaps it was that the breeze blew my energy her direction. I smile. I am blessed with a good smile. Good teeth. Good facial bone structure. My blue eyes sparkle when I want them to, and at this moment they flash! She returns the favor by turning on her own sparkle. I lean left and take another picture, giving her a quick signal to turn her head to the side that was not faux pas faux hair–ish. I use two fingers instead of one. She gets the message. Employees of the Mouse all understand the two-finger point and I know she was once an employee—I mean cast member—at the Mouse's House. Now she thinks I was also and that makes us familiars. It is a lie I will never need to defend. This will be a good picture. Which, if sold, is also a lie I will never have to defend. But it may get me another gig.

The band is talking about the old days and making surfing references that I do not completely understand, but I listen to them and pick up a few words here and there. You know, "gnarly" and "dude" and such, but that isn't true surf lingo anymore. "Shred." "Tubular." Those still are viable, but it sounds hollow if a landlubber like me tries to use them. The slanguage changes fast and I don't even swim. I respect the culture by not trying to fake it.

Some phrases I really like: "Girl in the Curl" is a good one. I commented to someone that I liked it and that got me a gig as photographer for a book release that covered the whole "real Gidget" crowd. That was fun because some of the women attending were very real and very true. A rare and surprising quality. They weren't promoting anything but the idea that girls, women really, but they said "girls" so I did, too, should be treated equal in all things and surfing was the place to begin. It was a weak argument, but the wine served there was nice and the pictures were pretty natural. Plus I got to meet the real Gidget. She's sweet.

My lens finds the one guy in the band who was the writer of the cowritten one-hit wonder, and I move in on him, making myself obvious. He is not as much of a pro at the publicity thing and seems more annoyed at my presence than the famous famous does. I think I "harshed his mellow." At any rate, he seems to be rambling, and his drummer, waiting to perform the famous solo, makes a couple of rolling riffs on the cymbals. It sounds swishy, like the surf, and I switch the direction of the lens to him. He likes it and twirls the sticks. The lead guitarist gets jealous and wants the camera back on him so he launches into the song. The band, pros and probably studio musicians and not the originals, no matter how tenuous the connection, launch in with nary a pause or dropped beat. And they rock it! I focus on the guitarist's hands as he draws the solo out. Each member has a turn as soloist, just like jazz, but surf beat.

The famous famous makes her way to the front of the patio and does some pose dancing, for which I oblige and shoot a string of provocative shots. Her wig is in place and secure enough, but I note she does not do many head movements. Her assistant stands back, looking chastened and chagrined. He probably delivered the errant hair alarm to her and now is the messenger to be killed.

Taking pix is easy. The crowd never grows unruly. The band grows weary. They are all on Social Security and Medicare. Probably medical marijuana, too. The buffet opens and I shoot some promo before the artistic layout is demolished by those seeking the free lunch. Of course it is not free, and while people straggle about with their faux fancy plates made of material stiffer than a paper plate but not quite as durable as plastic, and biodegradable, even though trees still were cut down to make the garbage, and petroleum was used to transport the future garbage, and the recycle company does not want the garbage if there was food on it. Still, everyone feels justified about using this disposable dinnerware because the recyclable stamp is clear on the bottom of the future garbage that everyone carries around with their California Cuisine piled high.

California Cuisine—just add an avocado.

The promoter announces the amount of money raised for "the cause," and to be honest, I am not paying attention. The camera is doing its duty and the promoter will be unhappy with the pictures no matter what. He just does not see himself as an aging surfer. The waxed and styled hipster mustache looks awkward on his fifty-plus, paunchy, balding, faux Tommy Bahama–shirted body. I can only do so much. I have a good camera.

The famous famous walks past me and says, "I look forward to see-ing those pictures you took. Talk to Nigel and he'll give you contact info. He's from England." She turns on her smile once more. I shoot a few close-ups and say thank you. She laughs as if it is funny, and I suppose it is. She does not seem to recognize me at all. It may be some secret agreement. Today we are both VIPs and she is more VI than I.

Nigel is quick to make amends to his mistress and hands me his card, her card, and the company card as if the multitude of paper will secure my personal promise of attention. He says softly, "She wants to see the pictures. I mean she really wants to see your work. But, you understand, only the ones of her." I nod affirmatively. I get the mes-sage. Then he actually leans close and whispers, "Her photographer didn't show up." There is real fear in his eyes.

They depart first: So sorry, another engagement; you know how it is when you are in demand, et cetera. The illusion of success. The crowd senses that the party is over and dissipates like the morning marine layer.

The band breaks down their own equipment and the buffet be-comes empty after the last stragglers grab "to go" leftovers, of which there is not much. Except for the free wine from the local business. It is awful, but free, and there is a banner that promotes the product. Even surfers have their standards. "Swill," says one as he tastes a dubious pinot grigio from a plastic wineglass. He wears baggies from his own clothing line and they are pretty nice according to the informal-formal surf dress code. His flip-flops are leather looking, and I recognize them from the display in his store.

He looks at me and smiles in recognition. "Hey, you're the guy from—" and I cut him off, agreeing, but not revealing the secret.

"Yes, I am! How are you? Is your business doing well?"

"It can always be better, but it's all good. I didn't know you do photography. We should talk; I need some promo shots from around the store."

"No worries. I have always liked the store layout and there are some really good pix waiting to happen. I'll even cut you a deal since we know each other." That last bit gets him, but he does like the compliment about the store.

Our social connection is tenuous. Before he can put me off, I say, "Are you in tomorrow? I am off and can stop by anytime that is convenient."

His face goes blank. "Sure. Try me tomorrow. I have a few things, but if you catch me in the morning, we can go over some ideas I have." And there it is. The California Promise.

Except I will be there. I want the job. I want the pay. I want to be a photographer and hang out at events where there are famous famous sons and daughters and trust-fund babies. And maybe even get to the point of attending the red-carpet openings with real stars and real cuisine and actual wine that is sold and not given away in the hopes that the little people will see it and buy it for the cheap price and faux prestige.

I am off tomorrow, but the following day I will be back in the produce section stocking the avocados again. Awesome health insurance, a 401(k), and a steady paycheck. The famous girl with the blond wig will come in to the store and she will remember where she knows me from. She will be more natural then: no wig, no eye makeup, no need for a photograph. And I will be real with her. I'll speak softly and show her some of the photos and treat her as an equal. We will conspire and maybe she will get me a gig at her next event. Maybe I will get her an invitation to my next photography gig. But no promises. And I will save her some special avocados because she is special and we are both vegan. When it is convenient.

The sun is setting. I take some shots that will be fantastic. But they will look like every other beautiful sunset picture taken from the beach, from the pier, from near the pier, or from pulling over on Pacific Coast Highway. The patio is now empty except for hotel employees acting out their roles. No one is looking at the sunset over the ocean. Why bother? There will always be another perfect day. There will always be another magnificent California sunset over the ocean. I promise.

The Quest for Avalon

Catheryn Hull

Glendora, California, 1970

I smelled the cigarette smoke first. And then a low laugh came from my right, followed by, "What's a matter, mama's boy? Scared to go to school 'cause you didn' do yer homework?"

He laughed again, louder this time, and then I saw him.

I stood up fast. I knew trouble when I saw it.

He was older than me, could be fifteen, taller than me but real skinny and ropy-like. His brown hair was shaggy and long like the Beatles but greasy looking. He leaned on a battered flat shovel, the kind you use to muck out a stable.

"It's none of your business why I'm here," I said, backing away from him.

"'It's none of your business why I'm here,'" he repeated in a girly voice.

"I didn't see any fences or signs saying to keep out. I can be here if I want."

"That's where you're wrong, mama's boy. Man who owns this orange grove pays me to keep little shits like you outta here."

I couldn't help but look up at the tree I'd been sitting under. The light rain had stopped. The lingering clouds acted like a giant magnifying glass, turning the sun's rays into laser beams that made the leaves so shiny and bright they hurt my eyes. I'd been in California a month, and this was the first orange tree I'd seen. But there were no oranges, just blossoms and little green balls the size of BBs hanging on the branches.

"Fine," I said. "I'll leave." I walked around him and headed toward the narrow dirt road I'd taken when I'd decided to ditch school. Some of the worst kids in junior high lived on my block, and this morning they were hanging out on the corner smoking, even though it was raining. I'd decided to take the long way to school, and that's when I'd seen it.

"That there is a private road," the creepy kid said, "owned by the man who pays me."

"I'm just passing through." I started uphill.

He was in front of me in an instant, holding the shovel handle across his chest as if to block me. "You ain't goin' nowhere," he said, and then he grinned, showing gray teeth that were green along the gums.

I ran for it.

I made it twenty feet up the road before he tackled me to the ground. My face hit the dirt. He sat on top of me and went through my pockets, finding the twenty Mom had given me for lunch for the week.

"Hot damn!" He jumped off me, waving the bill in the air. "You can come up here anytime you want, mama's boy."

I got to my feet and rammed him at the midsection, catching him by surprise, as I grabbed for the twenty. But he recovered quickly and shoved the bill into the front pocket of his faded blue jeans, laughing like a donkey. "You got balls for a little shit, I gotta say, but you're gonna have to kill me to get that twenty back."

I backed off.

"And if you kill me, that goes on your 'permanent record,'" he said and laughed again.

I rubbed at the red clay on my face and looked down at my Oxford shirt and khakis. Both were smeared with clay red as blood. "Keep it," I said as I walked around him. "We'll call it a toll."

"You callin' me a troll?"

I looked back at him. Could he really not know what a toll was? I suppose it was possible. The last toll road we saw on our way out here from Connecticut was halfway across the country in Ohio or some-place like that. I kept walking.

A minute later he was back with his shovel.

I walked faster.

"This road ends at a river," he said. "Goin' north or west, you'll have to cross it, and it's runnin' full right now with snowmelt."

"I'll deal with it," I said. North was where I was heading.

"I know a way across it."

"I'll bet you do." I tried to walk faster, but the hill was getting steeper and the damp clay softer. Soon I heard the rush of water.

He was still following me. "Don't you wanna know where I'm goin' with this shovel?"

"To your gold mine?"

He punched me in the shoulder and laughed like a donkey again. "You're funny. Know that, schoolboy?"

"Keep your hands off me."

"I'll tell you anyway. I'm goin' to dig up a grave."

I didn't take the bait.

The river was only fifteen feet across, no more than a stream really, but it was running fast over dark rocks with strings of knotted green moss trailing like hair downstream. Upstream and down held no promise of an easy crossing. I sat on a rock that was steaming and warm from the sun and looked to the green foothills and purple mountains beyond. It's up there somewhere.

"Told ya," he said.

I nodded toward the stream and asked him if it was safe to drink.

"This time a year, should be. I usually drink from the faucets in the grove."

I knelt on the sandy bank and cupped my hands into the icy water. I took several long swallows and rinsed the clay off my face as he stood watching me, leaning on the shovel.

"What's your name," I asked, "Huckleberry Finn?"

"Finn? No Finns livin' around here. They call me Rascal."

America had just planted a flag on the moon, nearly everyone had a color TV now, and acres of stucco tract houses were marching up the foothills chasing off the old groves. How could this guy not know who Huckleberry Finn was? "Who calls you Rascal, your parents?"

He snorted once and sat on a rock.

After another long drink, I was ready to go. "You going to tell me how to get across this so-called river or do I have to find my own way?"

He stood, started walking upstream, and said, "This way."

I followed him for at least a half hour across the rocky riverbed to a curve where the river had eaten right through a hill. There was no way to continue except up and over the hill. Rascal headed toward a path beaten through the wet grass. Stepping-stones led upward to an overlook above the river. On top was a one-room building made of river rock and cement with a caved-in rusty brown corrugated steel roof. The single glass window had been shattered and the door busted in, probably by Rascal.

I went inside but came right out again. A messy beehive was dripping down the far corner, the bees flying in and out through the open roof. I caught a glimpse of a leaning woodstove, the stovepipe reaching to empty sky.

Rascal had gone over to a grassy area near the edge of the cliff and was digging. I sat on the cold cement stoop to rest.

When I walked over to him, he looked at me, grinning like a freak, his left eye drifting to the side. "Been saving this one," he said. "Take a look at the headstone. It's got flowers 'n' stuff on it. Must be a rich old lady with gold and diamonds and rubies."

I read the tombstone. "It's a baby," I said.

"Bullshit."

"What?"

"How you know it's a baby?"

He couldn't read! I read the tombstone out loud to him nice and slow: "Elsbeth Mary Stoddard. Our beautiful angel. Born October 2, 1899, died April 4, 1900."

Rascal continued digging.

His shovel hit something hard, like wood.

I don't know why, but that hollow sound ripped at my heart, nearly clawing it out of my chest. A volcano erupted inside me. I grabbed the shovel and ran to the side of the cliff.

"What the hell you doin'?" he yelled.

He was on my back in an instant trying to get the shovel. I managed to shrug him off and drop it over the side. He grabbed my arms from behind. I slammed the back of my head into his face. I felt more than heard his nose give, and his warm blood poured down the back of my neck. When he let go of me to grab at his face, I ducked away and started running.

Of course he caught me. With the blood buzzing in my ears and my eyes all blurry, I fought him like a maniac, both of us rolling around in the wet grass. "What kinda monster are you?" I screamed. "He was just a baby."

I used my fists, my knees, my elbows, my teeth. I even scratched his face like a girl and nearly bit a piece of his ear off. He got in some good punches, but I barely felt them. I raged over and through him like a wildfire.

Eventually he started letting off. I kept at him until he rolled away and just lay there. "What's the matter with you?" he said between gulps of air. "He's dead. He don't know nothin' going on."

I sat up. My lower back ached where Rascal had punched me several times.

He remained on the ground. "And I thought you said the name was Elsbeth *Mary*. That's a girl's name. Even I know that."

He was right.

"And her parents must not a cared too much about her or they wouldn't have left her out here all alone."

I gulped air, trying not to cry. "And you're just making it worse by digging her up."

He ignored me. He got up and walked over to the edge of the cliff where I'd dropped his shovel. "And lookit that. How the hell am I gonna git that shovel back? It ain't even mine."

I lay back in the soft wet grass and took deep breaths. I thought about the little brass urn that my parents had carefully unpacked and placed on the fireplace mantel of our new home. As if we would ever have a fire in California, or snow, or bonfires in the woods in the fall, or friends I'd had since kindergarten, or a horse like Mandy. There would never again be a horse like Mandy. "We need a new start, Son," my father had said over and over again. "Someplace that doesn't remind us of all we've lost."

"Hey, what's-your-name, give me a hand," Rascal called out from somewhere down by the river.

He'd gone down for his shovel and kept slipping as he tried to climb up the slope. He must have slid into the water because his pants were wet up past his knees.

He held the shovel handle toward me. "Just hold on to this until I can get a footing."

I had to scoot on my belly and lean over the edge to reach it. Twice he nearly pulled me over the side.

By the time Rascal got to the top we were both spent. He flopped down onto the ground and started shaking all over. I pretended not to notice.

Once his breathing evened out, I said, "Scott. My name is Scott."

"Humph." He closed his eyes.

"You live around here?" I asked.

No reply.

"Where are your parents?"

I didn't think he was going to tell me, but without opening his eyes, he said, "Never knew my dad. My mom moved us out here from Missouri and left me with Grandpap till she could git famous in Hollywood." Another humph.

"So you live with your grandfather?"

"Did up until he died."

"So you live out here all by yourself?"

"For now," he said.

He must still think his mother was coming back for him. I didn't think so.

I stood and walked to the edge of the cliff and looked up and down the river. "You tricked me," I said. "There's no way to cross here. You just wanted me to help you dig up that little baby."

"Not a baby anymore," Rascal said and then sat up. "Just a box a bones. Why you so fired up to git across that river anyway? Nothing there 'cept more like this."

No way would I tell him about the rainbow I saw this morning. He'd call me crazy, and maybe he'd be right. A pot of gold at the end of the rainbow, just over that hill. I thought about King Arthur's magical island of Avalon where Excalibur was made, where food grows by itself and people live to be over a hundred and babies don't just die in their sleep for no reason. And Jason and the Argonauts and Don Quixote, all of them looking for something. Or someplace, like my parents, looking for a new start.

I walked back to Rascal. "Have you been over there?"

"'Course. I been everywhere 'round here, seen everything a million times."

"Maybe I'll see something you missed or that wasn't there before." He snorted.

I turned back to face the river and the foothills beyond. What would I do with a pot of gold anyway? Seems like it would be too heavy for me to carry home. And I doubt it would make my parents happy again or get my baby brother back or Mandy. Besides, our new place didn't have a barn.

For some reason, just knowing it could be there was good enough for me right now. It was certainly better than finding out it wasn't. I turned back to Rascal. "Are you really going to dig up that little baby?"

"Oh Christ." He flopped back down. "No. I will not dig up that little baby."

"Promise?"

"Promise. But I still think you're a little shit."

I was smiling as I headed toward the pathway leading down the hill. "I'll be back when the river's down," I called out to him.

"Bring your lunch money *and* your allowance." He laughed.

I looked back but didn't see him. He'd disappeared in the tall wet grass.

The Unpleasantness in Room 27A

Dana Hammer

A motel is probably the worst place to murder someone, except maybe a police station. Getting rid of a body requires preparation, precision, and above all, privacy. When you kill someone spontaneously on a scratchy floral comforter with a pillow, while surrounded by tired tourists in the rooms next to you, you've pretty much screwed yourself out of all of those things.

I sigh. This asshole has really made things difficult for me. And for himself! If he had just showed me a little respect and common decency, we wouldn't be in this situation right now. He could have died an old man in a comfortable hospital bed, soothed by the trickle of morphine, surrounded by his loved ones. Well, maybe not that last part. He was an asshole; he probably didn't have a lot of loved ones. Still.

When I asked him to come back to this room with me, this was not how I imagined things working out. I thought it would be a nice interlude in my little vacation, a little fun to spice things up. But the turdgobbler had to go and call me names like I'm some kind of common gutter floozy, and now look what's happened! I'm stuck with a dead body and no way to get rid of it. At Disneyland. The Happiest Fucking Place on Earth.

I take a quick peek out the window, pulling aside the thick beige drapes. It's so glaringly, annoyingly sunny! I can see a family of fat people waddling down the lane, looking stupid in their Mickey Mouse ear hats. Dammit.

I briefly think about calling the police. I could make a case that it was self-defense. Say he tried to attack me. It would be believable. I'm a small woman, and he's a big man. I was just a lonely tourist wanting to have some fun at Disneyland, and I was taken in by this sexually deviant predator. I was forced to defend myself.

But I know this won't hold water if anyone looks at my story too deeply. I have no marks on me to indicate I've been attacked. And after I smothered him with the pillow, I had a little fun with my pocketknife—which in retrospect was pretty stupid, but sometimes I get a little carried away. The point is, it would be hard to argue self-defense if anyone saw how I carved him up.

I set a sheet down on the ground and roll the guy onto it. He lands on it with a moist thud. I drag the body to the bathtub, which is much harder than you'd think. Dead bodies are heavy, much heavier than live bodies, because they just sort of sink into the floor, their blood pooling into the bottom of them, all viscous and thick. I worry about his fluids dripping out through the sheet.

After I get him maneuvered into the tub, I have to sit down to rest. I'm sweaty and gross, and I desperately want to take a shower, but since the tub is occupied, I'm out of luck. Now it's time to come up with a plan.

I've got him into the bathroom, which is probably the most important thing, because I'll be able to clean up after him easily. I yank the sheet out from under the body and put it in a shopping bag, which I then put into my duffel bag. I'll have to dispose of it in a Dumpster somewhere and set it on fire. Then I just have to get rid of the actual body. I'm thinking I'll chop it into smaller parts, bag them, and dispose of them bit by bit in the ocean. It shouldn't be too hard to rent a boat. I'll just say I want to do some fishing or something. California has lots of boats and opportunities for water fun!

The thing is, I already bought my park-hopper day pass for Disneyland and California Adventure. I posted this morning about how excited I was to go and about how I was going to post my pictures later in the day. Which means I have to get some pictures, or my friends and family will start asking questions.

So I'll head to the hardware store and pick up the necessities. Plastic bags, ropes, things like that. Then I'll head to a good kitchen supply store and get a butcher's saw. After I've got all my supplies, I'll make a stop at Disneyland. Then I'll come back to the hotel and take care of Mr. Disrespectful.

Disneyland is truly the Magic Kingdom!

I shriek with glee as the hologram tells me "Dead men tell no tales" on the Pirates of the Caribbean ride. I clasp my hands with joy as I watch the little movie made just for the Indiana Jones ride. I laugh at all the jokes the boat driver makes on the Jungle Cruise. And I eat three elephant ears, which makes me sick to my stomach, but I don't care because this is the most fun I've ever had!

The Tower of Terror is probably the highlight of the whole trip. I've always been a *Twilight Zone* fan, and this is a whole ride inspired by it! And it's done so well! I love how intoxicating it is to be lifted and dropped, lifted and dropped, over and over again, while people scream with joy and fear all around me.

I think the ride on the tram leaving Disneyland might be the saddest moment I've experienced in a long time. I want to live at

Disneyland. I want to set myself up in one of those top-floor apartments you see, or better yet, in Cinderella's Castle! I want to ride rides and eat elephant ears every day for as long as I live!

But I can't. Nope. I have to go back and take care of a dead body. I shudder to think of the stench. He's been sitting in a small room in the hot California climate this whole time. I can't imagine it's going to be poppin' fresh in there. I sigh. I should have picked up some air freshener. I hope the bleach I bought will take care of the worst of the smell.

Weary, I unlock the door to my hotel room. I set down all my packages, purchased with cash, of course. Then I go into the bathroom.

He's not there.

Not just not there, but there's no trace of him. No blood. No mess. No signs that anyone had ever been there at all. It's spotless.

Panicked, I go back out to the bed, where I killed him. He's not there. What the hell? Did I come into the wrong room?

I check my room key and I check the room number and I know that I am absolutely in the right room and that this is it. My clothes are still here in the suitcase, where I left them. This is my room.

So where the fuck is the body?

Did someone come in here and find him? Room service doesn't come until morning, I'm sure of it. And if someone found a dead body in a hotel room, they'd call the police. They would be here now, waiting to arrest me. They wouldn't just clean up the mess and leave. Would they?

Now I'm seriously freaking out. I wish I'd never laid eyes on that stupid prick. Or at the very least, I wish he'd never called me a cunt. Then I wouldn't have had to kill him. For God's sakes, this is like Jamaica all over again, except that time the body had the decency to stay put.

I quickly pack all my stuff into my suitcase. Whatever is happening here, I need to get out, and quickly.

Except I can't. The room is locked.

Frustrated, I try my key, to see if it's somehow locked from the inside. My key doesn't work. I pull on the door, yanking hard. Nothing happens.

I go to the window and find that I can't open it. It's sealed shut.

Now I'm panting and my palms are sweating. I pick up the phone to call the front desk and find there's no dial tone. What the fuck?

I grab my phone and find that it, too, is dead. I plug it into the wall, but that does nothing. It's as if the wall sockets don't work.

I press my face up against the window. I see more jolly fat people walking by and I shout at them. "HELP!" They don't hear me.

I start to see spots and realize I'm hyperventilating. I don't care. I have to get out of here, and I have to get out of here RIGHT FUCKING NOW. I grab the phone and bang it against the glass. I'm gonna smash my way out.

But that doesn't work. I try using a chair, hurling it against the glass with all my might.

Nothing.

I've worked up quite a sweat by this time, and I go to the sink to get a drink of water. I need to calm down and think rationally. There is a way to get out of here. I just have to think about it.

The tap doesn't turn on.

I scream. I tear at my hair. What the ever-living fuck is going on here? Is this some sick game? Some kind of terrible joke? Did the police find the body and now they're just messing with me before they arrest me?

Finally I sit back down. The thing is, yes, this situation sucks. But it is, by necessity, temporary. After all, checkout is tomorrow. The maids will come tomorrow morning and let me out. They have to! I just need to calm the hell down and wait until then. It'll all be fine.

I grab the remote, deciding to watch some TV in the meantime. It doesn't turn on.

And the maids don't come. Not the next morning, or the next.

I sit on the bed, trying my phone over and over again. I shout out the windows some more. I eat the candy from my purse, but it doesn't help stifle the intense hunger and thirst. The heat is oppressive, and with no air-conditioning, it's intolerable.

I pace back and forth, trying my phone, banging on the door, banging on the walls of the rooms next to me, but nothing works, and nothing changes. Finally, I'm too tired and sick to bang and yell, and all I can do is lie on the bed and wait. For what, I don't know.

From: Nelson Tompkins
To: All Staff
Re: Room 27A

Hello,

I'm sure by now most of you have heard of the unpleasantness that occurred in room 27A. Please know that it is all being handled by the authorities. We have been informed that the woman found in the room was a transient who died of a drug overdose. We are looking into what might be done for her family and ways in which we might be of assistance.

Please refer any media inquiries to myself or to your supervisor. Do not discuss any of the happenings with the media yourself. In addition, I trust that you will all handle this topic with discretion when discussing it with your friends and that you will not engage in rumor-mongering or pointless speculation. We at the Disneyland Motel are a family, and we look out for one another. I know that our mission is as important to you as it is to me.

Let's all remember our company motto: At the Disneyland Motel, there is only happiness.

Sincerely,

Nelson Tompkins
General Manager
Disneyland Motel

The Untimely Death of Sweet Mims

David Putnam

Bub's head whipped around to face Wendell. "Hey, I'm not gonna tell ya again, quit twirlin' that gun before you drop it and blow your balls off."

Wendell twirled the gun one more time. "They're my balls, ain't they?"

"Yeah, as little as they are, they're still all yours, but someone can walk by and see the gun and ruin this whole deal for us. You said yourself, deals like this don't come along every day, so lower that dang thing."

Wendell stuck the gun under his leg on the seat. The hot morning sun bore down on the truck. Blow sand speckled the sides and windows in surges, obscuring the street. Not many folks moved around in Barstow, not enough jobs, not enough money anymore. Too hot with the drought and the wind.

Bub counted, making it only to three before Wendell used both index fingers to tap out something on the dash of the truck, some inane tune from somewhere deep in his addled brain, humming to himself, burning off nervous energy.

"Wendell, stop. Come on, man, gimme a break, would ya?"

Wendell stopped. "Why you gotta be that way? I'm the older brother and you're always giving me orders like you're my daddy or somethin'."

"Someone's gotta be your daddy, ya big-headed buffoon."

Wendell shot Bub a hard glare and held it there.

"All right, I'm sorry. Just give it a rest, would ya? Just sit there and be still. We only gotta wait a few more minutes."

After a long moment Wendell broke his glare. He looked out the window and across the street to the Summit Savings and Loan situated in their little town of Barstow, California.

"Hey, I'm sorry. I didn't mean that big-headed buffoon thing."

Wendell wouldn't look at him.

Bub said, "Wendell, why don't you tell me what you're gonna do with your share of the money?"

Wendell's head swung around, a huge smile on his flat, pie-pan face. "You're not gonna laugh? You promise you're not gonna laugh?"

"Have I ever laughed at you?"

The question stumped Wendell as he took a moment to think it over.

"Hey, I've never laughed at you. I only laugh with you—you know that."

"Oh, right. I gottcha."

"Go on, then, tell me."

"All right. All right. I've a mind to pack it all up and move on down to Florida."

"Florida? Really?" This was the first Bub had heard of the plan.

"Yeah, buy me a shark-fishin' boat."

"A what?" Bub turned away to face his window so Wendell wouldn't see his smile, Wendell knew nothin' about no shark fishin'.

Wendell shoved him in the back. "See? That's why I don't tell ya nothin'. You make fun of everything I wanna do."

"No, no, really, go on. Tell me. I wanna know. No, I gotta know, 'cause if it's somethin' good, I might move on down there my ownself."

No chance in hell, but he needed to make Wendell believe it. He needed Wendell on his side at least for a few more minutes. But who was he kidding? He loved the hell out of his older brother, and if Wendell went to Florida, he'd have to go, too, jus' to keep him out of trouble.

"Really, Bub? Really? You're not messin' with me, are ya? Geez, I thought you was mad at me after what happened. You and me on a shark-fishin' boat, that would be tops, wouldn't it?"

"Yeah, really. I'm tellin' ya true. I can't stick around here, not after what you did to Mims."

The mention of Mims tarnished Wendell's smile. "I told Grams I was sorry about ol' Mims. And, Bub, I *am* real sorry about ol' Mims. Didn't mean for it to happen that way. You know that, don't ya? You know I didn't mean it."

"Done's done. Go on, tell me all about Florida."

Wendell's smile lit off again, huge and bright. "This good ol' boy from down Tulsa way was visitin' Florida, shark fishin'. You believe it, he went all the way down there to catch hisself some sharks. And I guess he hooked one of them monsters, one the size of a small Ford pickup, I kid you not. Took him the better part of a day to get him up to the boat. Took five of them crewmen to use them long poles with hooks to get that bad boy on board."

"You're kiddin' me."

"No, I'm not. This thing was huge, I'm tellin' ya. And you know what they found when they cut it from butthole to gullet?"

"What?"

"*Some dude's arm.*" Wendell's eyes went wide as he waited for Bub to react in kind.

"Naw, now you're yankin' on my dick."

"Nope, some dude's arm. I'm tellin' ya."

Across the street, a man in a brown ratty suit, with banged-up wing tips, carrying a briefcase, walked up to the bank's front door, stuck a key in the lock, opened the door, and disappeared inside. Bub sat up straight. He reached under his seat and pulled out his daddy's old Colt .45 automatic, the one his daddy stole from the army, and stuck it under his leg.

"We goin', Bub? We gonna do it now?"

"No, you idjit. Grams said not until ten o'clock. We can't do it a minute before or one minute after ten. She was very clear 'bout that. Ten o'clock on the dot."

"Bub, but if it's a bank, why doesn't it open at nine like all the other banks?"

"Grams says because it's just a payroll and businessmen's bank, that's why. Businessmen sleep in and don't get up until late, so the bank doesn't need to be open till ten. Used ta open at nine, but it closed to regular people two years ago, remember."

"But if he's there now, why don't we jus' do it now and get it over with? I'm nervous as a bag a cats."

"'Cause Grams says we can't be sure the payroll for the stockyards will be there till ten o'clock straight up. Gotta be ten o'clock."

"How lucky was it that Grams found out about that big ol' money delivery and that she told us about it? Told us. How lucky was that, huh, Bub? Especially after that thing with Mims. She could a told Hank Daugherty, like she tells him everythin' else, give it to him to do. And he'd a done it without us, and kept all the money, too."

"Real lucky."

Sweat ran in Bub's eyes and stung. He wiped them and checked both ends of Cherokee, the main drag through town. Not many folks moved about that early on a Saturday morn. Most of the traffic came from the Iron Skillet two blocks down, just a few folks across the street. There still wasn't enough money to eat outside your own kitchen.

He pulled Grandpap's pocket watch Grams lent him, opened it, and checked the time. Seven minutes to ten.

"Bub, how come you get to hold the watch and you get Daddy's gun when I'm the older brother?"

Bub ignored the question and fought the urge to pull the .45 from under his leg and check the load one more time, make sure a round was down "the throat." That's what Grams had called it when she'd taken him out back and shown him how to shoot it. "Rack the slide and ram one right down the throat."

But he'd already checked it three times now.

Seven minutes. He had only seven more minutes to wait and hoped his stomach didn't cramp up any more than it already had. He stared at the door to the bank, concentrating. Never in all his life had he thought he'd be sitting in his truck outside a bank with a gun under his leg. Wendell had caused this fracas that jus' never seemed to end. Bub had his heart set on a hundred and twenty prime acres of grassland out by Hickory Creek. He'd been savin' up for it. Run a few head at first, build his own herd. No way could that happen now. No way.

The day after they'd buried Mims, Grams had pulled Bub into the parlor and closed the double doors. She took the Virginia Slim that hung from her wrinkled lips framed with red lipstick, like clown makeup on a dried-apple doll, and blew a mouthful of smoke, crowding him back a little. With the cigarette between her fingers, she pointed at him, jabbed at him. "That's it, Bub. I cain't take that nickel-dick for one minute more. You get him outta here, or I swear ta Gawd"—she moved in close, her breath wet with the sweet odor of bourbon and mulled cherries—"I swear ta Gawd I'll take care of him my ownself. You hear me? I'll do it. You know I will."

Wendell bumped Bub. "You know what else? Go on, ask me what else they found."

"Huh?" Bub said. "What are you talkin' about?"

"On that dude's arm."

"What dude's arm?"

"From the belly of the shark, Bub. The dude's arm they cut out of the belly of that shark down in Florida. Tampa, I think it was. You don't listen to a thing I say, do ya? The arm still had the dude's watch on it—you believe it?"

Bub slowly turned to look at Wendell.

"Yeah, that's right," Wendell said. "Now I got your attention, don't I? One of them Rolexes, the paper said it was, and listen to this. It was encrusted with diamonds. A watch encrusted with diamonds. Never heard of such a thing, have you? Shark fishin', of all the damn things, huh? Outta the belly of a big ol' mako."

"Now I'm callin' foul on that one right there."

"What? Why?"

"'Cause everyone knows there ain't no makos in Florida. Those sharks are from down in South Africa or some shit." Bub didn't know for sure, but he needed to get Wendell off this dumbass idea and get his head back in the game set to go in less than what? Six minutes now.

"I'm tellin' ya, I read it in the magazine."

"And I tolt ya before, those magazines at the checkout counter in the grocery aren't for real. All that shit's made up for boneheaded—" He caught himself before he finished.

Too late.

Wendell's smile fell. He looked out the window again. "No, you're right. I am the bonehead. We wouldn't be sittin' here if it weren't for me. Go on, you can say it. Go on and say it, Bub."

Bub let it go.

Wendell said, "You never did ask me what happened in the barn, day before yesterday, what happened with sweet little Mims, I mean."

"You said you didn't do it on purpose. That's all I need to know."

Wendell shook his head. "No, you gotta right to know, and I really need to tell ya. I been holdin' it in too long. When it happened, Grams wouldn't listen to anything I had to say. She jus' kept on screamin' at me. Screamin' and screamin'." Wendell held his hands to his ears and squinted his eyes shut. "Screamin' and screamin', like the world was comin' to an end."

Bub put his hand on Wendell's shoulder. Wendell eased up on it, opened his eyes. "Here it is," Wendell said. "I'm gonna tell ya the whole thing. Okay, Bub? Can I tell ya the whole thing?"

Bub nodded. "Sure, go ahead."

Wendell swallowed hard. "Okay, I went into the barn to fork some hay to Ol' Douglas. I picked up the pitchfork and turned to the hay pile, you know right there over in the corner? That's when I saw sweet Mims kind of off to the side behind me, not movin' a lick. I mean, she was as stiff as a damn board. At first I thought she was dead. Then I thought she was watchin' me. But when I followed her eyes, I saw what she was watchin'."

Wendell held up his hands two feet apart. "Bub, I'm tellin' ya, it was the biggest rat I've ever seen. Big as a damn possum. I swear it was. Just sittin' there hopin' Mims hadn't seen him. But the old girl had for sure. And old Mims, you'd a been proud of her, Bub. She wasn't afraid, not one wit. She slowly stuck one leg and paw out, then the other, movin' 'em one at a time. Ol' Mims, she was stalking that giant rat, hell-bent on havin' it for breakfast.

"Well, I couldn't let Mims have a go at that big ol' rat. That rat could bite a leg off Mims in one chomp. Then what would Grams have said, huh, Bub? What would she have said if I'd let sweet Mims get eaten by a big ol' monster rat? Grams woulda had a piece a my ass for it, no doubt about it. Right? Am I right?"

Wendell waited for Bub to agree before he could continue, so Bub nodded. "Go on."

"Well, I didn't move and Mr. Rat didn't move. But sweet Mims, she kept slowly movin' her legs one at a time, one at a time, like they was weighted down or somethin'.

"Then it all happened real slow-like. But it was really weird. It happened real fast, too. I mean, it's hard to explain. Mr. Rat jumped straight up in the air the same time sweet Mims leaped. It was like they both knew it was gonna happen before it happened. It startled me, Bub. And . . . I . . . I jus' . . . I mean, I jus' kinda struck out. I thought I got the rat. I did. But when I looked down at the end of the fork, there was sweet Mims asquirmin' and athrashin', makin' this horrible little squealin' noise, like some kind a stuck piglet. Made me sick right there all over my boots. Spattered my own boots but good. You believe me, don't you, Bub?"

"Of course I do. You tell me that's the way it happened, then that's the way it happened." Bub looked away from Wendell and out the truck window to watch the bank. Two long minutes passed as time continued to tick down. Like Grams had said, with the money from the bank Bub could go to Oregon, find hisself two hundred prime acres of land up that way, start over there. He asked Wendell, "What happened to the rat?"

After another moment passed, Bub looked away from the bank and over at Wendell.

Wendell stared out the windshield with a faraway look in his eyes. "Neoprene."

Bub looked at the bank and then back at Wendell. "What?"

Wendell turned and looked Bub in the eyes. "Why'd he have neoprene, Bub? The arm of that dude from in that mako shark's belly had neoprene on it. We gotta go somewhere, Bub. Grams wants to kill me. I know she does. It ain't right, but that's the way it is, and Tampa's as good a place as any."

"She doesn't want to kill ya. She gave us this great idea of hers, didn't she? Her best idea in years, hittin' the businessmen's bank like this jus' before payroll."

"Bub, we ain't bank robbers, not by a long shot."

Bub reached over and shoved Wendell's face. "Snap out of it. We gotta go in three minutes, and I'm gonna need you sharp. You with me, Wendell?"

"I'll always be with you. You know that, Bub. But why can't we jus' start up this here truck and head on down to Tampa? Forget all this mess and get goin' right now."

"And what are we gonna live on when we get down there, huh?"

Wendell's brilliant smile returned. "Haven't you been listenin' to anything I've been sayin'? I got two words for you, jus' two. Diamond . . . encrusted . . . Rolexes."

"Ya damn fool, that don't make any sense at all. You think there's a whole grip of rich fellas down there jus' walkin' around with one arm? I tolt ya not to read those dumbass magazines. Now, come on, let's go."

Bub got out of the truck so mad he could spit and didn't know why, not entirely. Why'd Wendell have to be that way?

The hot, dry wind blew sand and made it difficult to see too far ahead.

Behind him Wendell's door slammed, the sound muffled a little in the high wind and dust and loose trash swirlin' all around. Wendell followed along and caught up. "Okay, Bub, we still gonna do it jus' like we talked about. I watch the door while you do all the talkin', right? Don't know if I kin do anything but watch the door. I'm real scared. Don't think I kin even say word one, Bub, not word one."

All of a sudden the billow of sand parted. The air cleared, and there stood Marshal Floyd Dickerson, with his long head and thick, black-framed glasses, leaning over the top of a Winchester shotgun pointed right at them. Three deputies also armed with shotguns pointed their way stood beside him. There was enough double-aught buckshot in the four guns to blow them both to hell and gone.

"Damn, Bub. Damn. How'd they know? How the hell did they know?"

Bub whispered to no one, "Grams, why'd ya do it?"

Verity's Truth

Maddie Margarita

Alta California, Mid-1800s

Powerful Santa Ana winds howled through the hills outside of town, scorching the earth and rattling windows and doors in the Hair of the Dog before rushing to the Pacific Ocean.

Lanterns flickering dangerously above her, Verity Clark pulled another pint and stared out from behind the old oak bar.

Earthquake weather.

Maybe that explained it. Her almond-shaped eyes—one blue, one brown—noted every wobbly stool in the battered saloon was taken. Saddled with the survivors. Outliers—humans who from birth, or since the great quakes, possessed metaphysical and arcane gifts. Laughing or fighting. Cooling their boots along the tarnished brass rail. Mending frayed nerves with beer and whiskey.

Verity could smell their fear. She slid a beer down the bar. Not that she wasn't afraid. She was only a child when the first of two killer quakes struck, destroying most everything, save for the Hair of the Dog and a portion of the Mission San Juan Capistrano. The mission's Great Stone Church, once a refuge for Outliers, was brought to its knees. Only the modest Serra Chapel and Sacristy endured.

The earth's angry rumblings had divided an already divided town, pitting native Acjachemen against settlers, Outlier against Plain. A string of recent murders had only made matters worse.

"You heard the news, girl?" Floyd demanded.

Girl? Verity's head jerked up in surprise.

Half Acjachemen and half Mexican, she was called "Half-breed" by most people—even Outliers like Floyd. She was usually too busy tending bar, washing dishes, and shouting orders to Juan Carlos, the lazy cook, to notice what people called her—but not tonight.

"Another one's gone missing. Disappeared over near where the general store used to be." Floyd drank down his beer as Verity filled another. "That makes five since that last goddamned quake. And that goddamned sheriff still ain't done a damn thing about it."

The bodies of four girls, all around her own age, soulless and drained of fluids, had been found near the convergence of the three creeks. They'd all been Outliers like Verity and her grandmother.

"Do they know who she was? The girl?" Verity anxiously brushed straight hair the color of a raven's wing away from her face and then wished she hadn't. People seemed less nervous around her when she hid the thin, pink burn scar that started under her blue eye, continued over the bridge of her nose, and ended under her brown eye.

Floyd shook his head regretfully. "It was Corazon."

The glass slipped from her hand and shattered on the bar. Corazon was Tushmalum Helqatum—a Hummingbird Singer. Another Outlier. A finger of dread slid down her spine. Was someone, or something, hunting Outliers?

"Her grandmother's too sick to make it without her help," Floyd said, flicking his wrist so the broken glass fused perfectly together and floated between them. "Better make that two gone, I guess."

"Stop talking about her like she's dead," Verity snapped, plucking the glass out of midair. "If you're so worried, go out and look for her yourself."

Instead, Floyd commenced backslapping with the other Outliers and Acjachemen who congregated here to avoid scrutiny from the townsfolk.

The Hair of the Dog was one of the few places where they could gather without problems from Enoch Stewart, the town's young sheriff. Stewart's wife had been an Outlier, and one night, without warning, she took their baby daughter and ran. After that, the sheriff made it clear he would just as soon bar the door to the Dog, light a match, and watch them all burn.

Verity sighed and swore that would never happen. Not while there was breath in her body.

The front door suddenly blew open. Verity felt her heart race.

"Whiskey, please." Ben pressed his tight, flat belly against the bar but Verity already had a dusty bottle in her hand.

Tall for an Acjachemen, Ben was smart and kind, with a smile to soften even the hardest of female hearts. He was also a door to the spirit world, prone to violent possessions, and drank too much. Verity knew he used the liquor to stay numb, invisible. But it didn't seem to help. The spirits took turns wearing him like a cloak.

"You hungry?" Verity asked, ignoring the uncomfortable feeling in her stomach.

Her eyes saw more than most, except where Ben was concerned, and Grandmother's words came flooding back to her.

Your eyes are a mirror. Those who are dark inside will cringe when they look upon you, for their wickedness is reflected back to them. Those who are clothed in lightness will see your beauty.

"I could do with whatever you have left over," Ben said suddenly, focusing on her. "How was your day?"

Verity didn't look up at him, or into the small mirror above the large basin where she washed the dishes for his dinner. She needed no reminder that her eyes and scar were disconcerting, even to her.

"Verity? You okay?" Ben asked. "You've been scrubbing your fingers instead of the glass."

She glanced down. Her knuckles were raw and bleeding, and the bit of steel wool she had in her hand was dotted with slivers of skin. "Did you hear? About Corazon?"

Ben nodded and poked at the beans and rice she gave him. "We searched the cliffs and the beaches."

"She didn't just wander off. The bodies were found drained, Ben. Like something was feeding on them. Whatever took them can't be human."

"How can you be so sure?" He slowly lifted his head. "You of all people should know that people are capable of worse."

She'd been four, and asleep on the floor with her dog, the night someone tossed an oil lamp and a lit match into her mother's house. Verity traced the scar under her eyes. She'd awoken screaming as an acrid liquid splashed her face and arms and then caught fire. Screams echoing in her head, her face and arms bubbling and raw with burns, she'd rolled in her blanket, trying to put out the flames on her skin and on Bernardo's oil-soaked fur—but it was too late. Her dog was dead.

Verity couldn't change what happened to her, but maybe she could prevent something terrible from happening to someone else.

"I think I know how we can find out who took Corazon and the others." Ben's eyes were on her when she tucked the whiskey bottle back behind the bar. "But I don't think you're going to like it."

Ben gripped Verity's slender forearms. "It's not working."

Effort drained from his hairline and streamed down his face like January rain.

They'd moved to the dark end of the bar but Verity could see past his mask of frustration and into his heart. Ben had never willingly opened himself up to spirit—or human—and neither of them was sure what would happen when he did. All they knew was that Ben felt stronger when they were skin to skin.

"Try again." Verity watched nervously as Juan Carlos laid his knives out on the bar. "We don't have much time."

Freeing Juan Carlos from the kitchen to take her place—even for a few minutes—was risky but necessary under the circumstances.

"Settle your mind, Ben." Verity tightened her hold on him and closed her eyes. "Call to the spirit who possesses the answer we seek. Do it now."

Shutting out the wind and drunken laughter whirling around them, Verity let herself sway with the full rich sounds of the *vihuela*, the small guitar that strummed itself in the corner near the door. In her mind's eye, she could see the music. Drenched in burnt oranges and cool blues, she floated atop each haunting note. Chasing the intricate melody up and down, faster and then slower, until it narrowed into a single red thread. Afraid it would disappear, Verity reached for it and fell headfirst through the eye of a needle.

She felt the unnatural stillness before she heard it, and when she opened her eyes, Ben sat cross-legged in front of her. Above them, a million blue-white stars glittered against the relentless night. A crisp, white winter blanketed the desert floor and dusted the Joshua trees and high desert chaparral around them.

"Where are we? What's happening?" Verity watched as silvery crystals of hoarfrost hardened down her arms from her elbow where Ben's hands held her to the tips of her fingers.

"Ben!" she yelled into the darkness.

But when he slowly inclined his head toward her, it wasn't Ben. His brown eyes had rolled back until only the whites remained. Something primal urged her to run and break their bond. But her purpose was clear. She would never betray his trust. Verity drew strength from her fear and straightened her spine. "I secured this human host for you, Spirit. You owe me an answer. Where is the girl— Corazon? Who is hunting the Outliers. And why?"

"Too *many* questions." The spirit blinked. It had robbed Ben's face of its warmth and humor, but not its intelligence. "But not the one that torments your sleep."

Verity struggled not to look away. Somehow, the spirit knew she would give anything to learn Ben's true feelings for her. But information and favors were currency in the spirit world. She would need to be careful not to incur a debt she couldn't repay.

"Your eyes." The spirit stared at her. "And that mark on your face . . . has it always been there?"

"Stop wasting time. Where is Corazon, and who killed the others?"

"The mission is the bridge," was all the spirit said.

"The mission . . . in San Juan?" Verity craned her neck closer.

Spirits often spoke in riddles, but she wished this one would just come out and say what it meant. "What does this have to do with Corazon and the others?"

"It will become clear. In the meantime, allow me to help your friend."

"What do you mean?" Verity was even more confused.

"I am strong enough to ward off other spirits. Convince this mortal to let me stay in this body and I can make him love you. I can also give him something you can't. Peace."

What would that mean for Ben? Would he still be the same man she loved? Was this even possible?

Verity knew spirits were not only shrewd but notorious braggarts. "If you're so strong, why not just take him now?"

The spirit smiled mysteriously. "Remember, Verity Clark. Nothing unearned, or not freely given, ever truly belongs to the taker."

Was the spirit telling her that Ben didn't love her? Or that even if the spirit could make Ben love her, he would never be hers?

Verity felt dizzy, and when her head cleared, she was once more in the Hair of the Dog. Ben had collapsed on the bar in front of her. She grabbed a wet rag, then a bottle, and tended to him until he lifted his head.

"Where is Corazon? Did we find out who it was? What did I say?" Ben wiped beads of sweat from his upper lip with the back of his hand and took a strong pull from the bottle.

"The spirit wasn't clear. I'm sorry. Something about the mission being a bridge . . ."

"That's it? We're still no closer to finding Corazon?"

She shrugged uncomfortably. Not only had they failed, but she had a bad feeling they had opened the door to a lifetime of spiritual trouble for Ben.

Ben pulled himself off the stool and grabbed the dusty bottle off the bar. "I'm heading home."

This was no time to bring up the spirit's proposition.

Unsure if he was angry at her, she watched Ben shuffle past the now half-empty tables toward the saloon's front door. But something else was bothering her. By using Ben's body, the spirit had incurred a debt. It was honor bound to answer the question she'd asked. Had she missed something?

Verity thought back to the spirit's words. Her arms began to tingle.

The ground trembled as Verity crossed over the threshold into the mission's courtyard. This had to be it. The mission was the only place the spirit had mentioned by name.

The winds had shifted. Shrouds of ocean mist and pale moonlight hung off high stone walls and hovered above the mission's narrow stone walkways. Cool, moist air chilling her skin, Verity forced herself to move forward. Stepping quietly around plots of fragrant sagebrush and Spanish bayonets—she prayed she wasn't too late.

There was a muffled cry up ahead and she moved closer, drawn to a flickering of light outside the wall.

"This is the last one!" she heard a man growl. "That was our agreement."

Heart pounding, Verity pressed her back up against the tall, stone wall and then cautiously peeked around the corner.

Sheriff Enoch Stewart stood in the middle of the cemetery, his lantern illuminating gravestones and dark, freshly turned earth, along with a mane of wavy black hair.

The sheriff kidnapped Corazon and the other Outliers?

"There's no need for her to suffer," Sheriff Stewart said.

Terror and disgust churned like bile in her stomach. Verity felt helpless. She hadn't thought what she would do if she actually found the killer or that the killer might actually be someone she knew.

The sheriff lifted a sobbing Corazon to her feet. The ground shook like he'd opened the gates of hell and a keening erupted from the back of the cemetery. A sound so raw it vibrated in her chest. If Verity wasn't already frozen with fear, she would've fallen to her knees when an eight-foot-tall entity materialized in the glow of the sheriff's lantern. A shadowy being, first solid and then not, shifting in hues of gray and crimson, radiating its evil intent as it descended upon the screaming Corazon.

The sheriff jumped back, tripping on gravestones, and Verity heard a loud voice.

"Stop! Leave her alone!" Verity realized in horror the voice was hers and that she was standing in the middle of a moonlit graveyard.

The demon stopped to peer down at her, its eyes two monstrous, swirling pits. She knew she was going to die right after Corazon, but she would not go gently. Rooted where she stood, her grandmother's words circled in her head.

Your eyes are a mirror. Wickedness reflected back on the dark ones.

Her brown eye twitched even as the blue one drew in any and all particles of light from the night around them. The hair lifted from her scalp as power surged through her and she aimed the mirror of her eyes on the roiling tower of evil before her.

Scorched, the demon wailed, staggered back, and dropped Corazon to the dirt.

Disoriented and blurry eyed, Verity saw Corazon scramble away and waited for the sheriff to do the same. But he didn't.

"You did this," Verity yelled at the sheriff as he prepared to fight alongside her.

"You don't understand . . ." He struggled to regain his footing as the demon shook the earth beneath their feet. "I tried to kill it, but I couldn't. It promised to kill every soul in town if I didn't bring the Outliers. I had no choice."

The hungry demon roared. It wasn't interested in the sheriff's excuses either. Fully enraged, it advanced on them. Verity stood her ground, she thought of Ben, of what they'd just been through, and had an epiphany.

Nothing unearned, or not freely given, can ever truly belong to the taker.

"Release their souls and return to the hell you came from," Verity commanded, and her blue eye reflected the spirit's potent truth upon the demon until it was no more than a puff of sulfurous smoke.

Verity rubbed her eyes and turned toward the young sheriff.

"I know what you're thinking," he said. "But no matter what you say, no one's gonna believe I kidnapped those girls—or that you banished a demon in the mission's cemetery."

The truth was ugly sometimes.

"Maybe knowing I delivered those girls to their death is punishment enough." The self-loathing in the sheriff's words sliced through Verity's conflicted heart. But she was not here to judge, at least not tonight.

"I couldn't see it before," the sheriff said. "But there are things out there, evil things, that we all need protection from."

Verity could feel the sheriff looking at her—past her half-breed looks, the scars, her unmatched eyes—and she saw something new in his eyes. Respect.

She heard footsteps, and Ben was suddenly behind her.

"I had the strangest feeling." He eyed the sheriff. "Somehow I knew you were here and in trouble."

Worried that they'd somehow created a permanent connection by inviting the spirit into Ben's body, Verity stumbled.

Fully drained, and hopefully only temporarily half blind, Verity allowed Ben to lead her away from the sheriff and along the pathway out of the mission's cemetery. "What did you see?"

"The truth," Ben said, staring at her. "*You* are the bridge. Not the mission. It was a prophesy. You are half and half, Verity. The bridge between two peoples. Two worlds."

Rays of hazy sunrise slowly crept over the tall stone walls, making the night's events feel like a distant, half-forgotten nightmare. She didn't have the strength to think about the future.

"You've already built one bridge, Verity. You can't hide from destiny."

Verity thought about the sheriff and Corazon as a small flock of birds settled in the mission's alcoves.

"The swallows are back," Ben said, looking up. "I think it's a sign."

"Of what?" Verity asked.

Ben swung a heavy arm around her shoulders. "Hope."

You Can Bank on the Breeze

PJ Colando

The mortgage was due—since before Christmas—and my plans to secure sufficient funds hadn't flourished. Santa stiffed me, and my lottery tickets persistently lost. I was shit out of luck, hope-rope-a-doped, veering over the almighty edge. Perhaps a bank robber would lose a few hundred bills as he helicoptered away from a heist. A couple of Grovers in my hand would put me in good stead.

In 2006 I escaped Barrio Las Flores, tatted elbows to wrist, glad to be alive. My woman lured me, applied her charms. Soon I palmed the keys to a house, lock-stepped to a mortgage as well as a wife. As always, there was good with the bad, bad with the good. Point of view matters; the rest slides.

The baby required constant coddling, diapers, and food. My wife was skinny and discontent, except when breastfeeding the kid. Guess where that left me? Closer to the schemes of former homies tugging on my soul.

Our two-year-old preferred to cavort diaperless, so he scattered waste across our home's slender side yard, fertilizing the lawn we couldn't afford. We'd envisioned lantana, red geraniums, and tall palm landscape to mimic the developer's brochures. Now our neighbors surmised we owned a pet.

We don't. The baby and toddler trade yelps while my wife barks at me.

Once upon a time we owned a tabby that tiffed with its own nose rather than merely lick and preen. The independent cuss abandoned us after slinking under our flimsy wood fence to explore greener turf. Some neighbors housed a hapless, slow-moving dog in their scruffy backyard. The howler apparently allowed theft of his daily ration. Pugnacious won the meal.

I don't sleep much. I fret, worry, thrash, toss and turn to supplant the gym I can't join. Desperation fueled by determination to prevail in our recession-drained economy propels me past breakfast to work at the Anaheim Inn, an old folks home thirty miles from our new house. Interface with these genteel elderlies helps me miss my folks less. My parents died soon after we came to this country. Their funerals cost us the fortune they lacked, even in a barrio church.

Today is payday. I welcome the freeway slog in near dark. I volunteered for every overtime hour offered this month, so the check will be huge. The value of ferrying meal trays, listening to repetitive tales, and emptying bedpans increased, flowing with the constancy of biological functions. Like a store clerk's zest for constantly folding and refolding clothing cast aside by those eager to rifle stacks, to consider purchase of new, and then walk away. That's what my wife said about her intermittent shifts at Kohl's.

I marched into the boss's office pronto at 9:00 a.m., beaming, my hand outstretched. The check he retrieved from the safe felt better than a bro hug. I didn't open the sealed envelope to check the math. Didn't want to dis employer-employee trust; I craved continued overtime.

My workday demeanor pepped up with the paycheck. Pocketed in a white envelope I fondled constantly, it filled my cotton uniform with hope. I rushed about the facility, serving meals, sharing a smile, touching an old woman's cheek before I massaged her knees. My benevolence swelled beyond monetary reward with our stability earned. I felt commissioned by God to save the day for others and wore pay-it-forward like a badge. I hummed gospel tunes and romped through the halls.

A glance at my watch became ritualistic after my hand emerged from its frequent check caress. Too often, apparently, because Bonnie, my favorite coworker, accused me of Tourette's, like Mr. Jones in room 223. I'm the only one willing to serve the man who flings swear words, poop, and food at the walls. Bonnie figured I'd contracted the old man's syndrome.

At two seconds past 5:00 p.m., I punch my time card and jog to my beater at the end of the parking lot's single row. I've timed the lights along Lincoln Avenue to within a second of caution. The destination is my neighborhood bank, the holder of our home mortgage, the one that's open until 6:00, the one that freeway congestion seems to push farther away each day.

I smile at the face of a conquistador in the mirror: skin as brown as toast, gray-green eyes shaded by black brows, a 'stash under a nose ready to lead. I'm so thirsty I want to lick the sweat sliding in front of my ears, but it's not worth the time for tricks. I pull the Saint Christopher medal to my lips, watch it swing back, and bang the dashboard for luck.

Soon I've crossed several lanes to merge into the carpool, bluffing my way because it's Friday with its extra traffic loads, people heading to Vegas to bet it all on red to get back in the black. Since my lottery fails, I prefer safer fundraising, but a bank deposit is urgent, so I risked it.

I groove to the radio play of Prince, OutKast, Janet, and Jennifer Lopez, tossing my head as if I, too, had a mane. I used to, but buzz cuts, performed beside the kitchen table, don't require combs. I look and toil like a marine.

But I bob my head like the guitarist I used to be when I had wet dreams. Now I have a wife, a past-due mortgage, and two kids. I've got obligations to the tune of $330,000. Too many credit cards shuffling the debt, too many zeroes to absorb, too much to sweat. I'm going to be working through this life into the eternal, earnest to not punch the down elevator button.

I dive out of the carpool with precision-timed speed, swoop into the off-ramp, and turn, sans signal, onto the congested streets of Corona, California. I think the city's name means something like "the sun," which is about to go down. With sunset comes a drop in the temperature and a surge in the winds. It takes an hour for the ocean breezes, the coastal cities' coolers, to sweep into our dingy streets.

I roll down my car window—yes, you read that right—my beater's windows have a crank that moves them up and down. It's a lot to manage, turning the handle with a nondominant hand without wrenching one's arm out of its socket. My right hand longs to assist its twin, but it sticks tight to steering. Otherwise, the car will wander, making both hands' efforts pointless. Because I'd be dead. Does my life insurance have a suicide clause?

But I digress.

Ah-h-h. Cool success. Ease the pace on the gas. The breeze flutters hope at my face. My eyes tear. My accomplishment is in sight. I'm only two blocks away from saving my home.

I scoot into the drive-up banking lanes, amazed at the absence of a line. God has greased my path. The kiosks save time, no bank entry required. Instead a sleek, secure drawer glides out with a slide-back top, like a small sarcophagus for my money, a tomb of safety until the check achieves the bank's stamp: "DEPOSIT."

Timing is everything, and it's lickety-split, drama unintended by me, fueled by an economic threat. The goal is to replenish the account upon which I wrote an exorbitant check and dropped into the overnight slot this morning: four months past due, but a payment on our account. I'm feeding the mortgage monster, anticipating grace.

Sally—the clerk's name tag is in overlarge caps—smiles and voices a muffled, "Hello. Welcome to First Third Bank." Her big-beaded necklace bounces as she presses the controls to extend the robotic drawer. I put my car in park and dig into my pants pocket for the now-pleated envelope. I clutch it and tug. The cheap paper catches in my uniform's crotch creases, and I nearly rip the treasure as I attempt to slide it out. I don't breathe until its release. I stabilize the heels of my hands on the steering wheel, insert my index finger under the flap, and lift.

The check appears and my watch fairly shrieks, *No time for ceremony. Fork over the check!*

I slide the check out, lift it over the lip of my car, and—the wind catches the check just as I drop it toward the bin!

It floats across the beater's windshield. My hands stab at the wiper controls in a vain effort to deputize them for the retrieval task.

My hands fall to my chest, where my heart blasts its alarm. My body is in flight-or-fight mode, to mirror the check that's gone air-mail. *Zoom-zoom.*

I attempt to open the car door, but the drawer blocks my exit. I swear, edge forward a few feet, and slam the car into park. The damn wipers are still moving—*fwap-fwap-fwapping*, scraping across a dry and dirty windshield in sync with Gloria Estefan.

I clamber out of the car, no small matter because, despite wearing one all my life, I've forgotten to unclip the seat belt. By the time I fully emerge, the check is out of sight.

I wheel toward the back of my car, to get a larger sky view, and nearly gut myself with the drawer. My eyes jerk to the clerk window. Even from this distance, I see Sally's face flame and she quickly retracts the device.

I'm stumbling and tumbling, grasping at the door handles for ballast. Crap, my foam-soled oxfords have come untied. As I retie my shoelaces, my mind tries alibis on for size. I ponder anew if my insurance policies are current and harbor a suicide clause. I pray loudly to the Lord.

Maybe I blasphemed as I shouted, because two face-blanched bank tellers are soon by my side. Both women in three-inch heels, blouses with pertly flourished bows stuffed into firmly pressed slacks, as if neither had worked all day, seated on bankers' stools.

They pull me upright—into check-search mode—as if I weren't a one-hundred-sixty-pound fool, blubbering about mortgages and responsibilities, God's curses, and worse. Sally points this way and Juanita points that. I take the middle ground, glad for their help. We scamper about as fast as we can, heads tipped back, eyes benefitting from the binoculars of adrenaline.

Seconds, minutes, centuries go by. Dizziness threatens to overwhelm me.

My shoulders sag. I figure the check is in Vegas by now, saving another gambler's fortunes. I try to recall the names and addresses of homeless shelters. I am ready to rend my shirt.

Just then something flickers in the pepper tree, overgrown in the parking lot's sliver of sidewalk landscape.

Was it? Yes, a rectangle of rarified beauty: my paycheck, lofted like a child's birthday balloon to perch on a branch. The wind tussled and jostled, but the check held fast in a cluster of red berries. I'd always despised those berries, dispensed in squishy messes among the bird splats on our neighborhood's sidewalks. Now the berries reminded me of mistletoe, and I bear hug Sally while Juanita runs into the bank for a broom. To mask my embarrassment, I return to my car to kiss Saint Christopher.

Juanita returns with the broom, batting at the branches like a pro. The berries give up the check. It drifts like a parachute, but the wind snags its edge again. The chase is on! *Clickety-click, clomp-clomp* run. Our team cannot let the wind win.

Though it's after 6:00, the sky hasn't darkened yet. We watch the check, follow its path, its billowy dance through the breeze. Its trajectory proves short—and soon Sally, mimicking an outfielder's stretched-arm catch, retrieves the prize.

Sally smiles and encases the check in both hands. She places it in my open palm and stakes a fingernail to secure it, while she clicks open a pen and pops it into my other hand. I sign the check—holy jeopardy, I'd neglected that step—and both women scurry into the bank. I stand there, rooted like the pepper tree, heaving to breathe, the only human on the vast blacktop.

Within moments, I witness Sally's silent cheers and watch her wave a deposit receipt, framed by the bulletproof glass window as large as my car. The aluminum drawer slides out, as if from a space alien's craft. I open it, scoop the slip of paper from the bin, and stuff my pocket. I boost my grin, lob two kisses to the window after I fist pump, and head home, refraining from the parking lot doughnut my car's worn tires won't bear.

"Don't pay the ransom. I'm home safe," I exclaim when I burst into our rescued house a half hour later than late. Our home smells great! Hot tamales!

My wife drops her pout and slithers into my open arms to plant a giant smooch on me. The kids gape.

We'll dine tonight, though no family and friends will be invited to celebrate. Our cul-de-sac has emptied, neighbors leaving in the middle of the night, financial casualties falling like dominoes in a YouTube stunt. But our tiny family will not lose our American dream, impaled like others by wildly inappropriate mortgage practices.

I didn't realize bankers tortured innocents as much as barrio gangs, but I whoop-ass beat the bastards. I prevailed—and I will again.

You can bank on that.

Zolota: Another Gold Rush

Rose de Guzman

January 1838
Fortress Ross—Russian Settlement, 100 versts north of San Francisco

A lazy Sunday afternoon, the days still short in the middle of winter—a mild winter, compared to the harshness of Alaska, but winter nonetheless. The smell of beeswax candles still lingers in my nose and the chants from the morning's Divine Liturgy in the colony's wooden chapel echo down the California coast.

I draw my wool shawl, adorned with red flowers, closer around my body to push back the damp sea air. I hear hoofbeats and the sounds of whooping men. Could one of them be my brother along with the rest of the young men, gone these last two weeks on an expedition?

As they grow closer, I can make out what they are shouting. "*Zolota*—gold! We found GOLD!"

I hesitate, wanting to run into the house to tell my parents, but also wanting to run toward my brother, my suitor, and the others. What have they found in those faraway hills?

The next thing I know, people are rushing out of their houses and toward the walls of the fort as Ivan leads the men inside. Excited whispers among the crowd turn into shouts—if there is anyone in the entire settlement who does not know that our men have found gold, they must be deaf or fools.

I run toward the stockade, almost sliding through the south gate as the men ride through the west gate.

Ivan rides up to me, and before I know it our father is right there as well.

"Is it true?" our father asks, cutting out all the pleasantries you would expect when a man's only son returns.

Ivan nods. "And quite a bit of it, too—more than enough to turn things around for us here."

My father looks solemn. There are fewer sea otters than there used to be, and the fur trade is struggling more than anyone wishes to admit.

Another man rides up beside us—Sergei, the man who has been courting me for a few months now. He could use a shave, and his breeches are dirty and torn, but his eyes sparkle with adventure and anticipation.

He has not spoken to my father about marriage—he needs to save money for our future together, or so he says. I would marry him with nothing and live in a hut, but he insists that I deserve better.

"Where was it?" my father asks Ivan.

Ivan shakes his head. "Later." He almost mouths the words.

"Who found the gold?" My father cannot wait to hear the whole story.

Ivan points toward Sergei.

Sergei found the gold?

Does that mean, then, that it belongs to him?

To us?

Can we marry, sooner rather than later, perhaps even before the Great Lent begins? Maybe even before the visiting priest goes on his way again?

Before he even says a word, Sergei reaches deep into his saddle-bag and pulls out a golden nugget the size of my thumb.

I reach for it, but I pull my hand back just before I touch it.

"Oh, Larissa, there is so much more there. You can't even imagine how much gold."

I feel my eyes grow wide. "But who . . . who does it belong to?"

I can see my father's mind spinning. "That will need to be . . . decided, won't it? But I am sure there will be some reward for the man who found it." He gives me a knowing look. My father is a craftsman, but he has the ear of the fort's commander. I somehow doubt that they have plans for anything like this—which means anything goes, or so I hope.

The settlement is abuzz the rest of the afternoon, as the story of the gold's discovery is told and retold, and the nuggets are locked away in a safe in Commander Rotchev's office. As for Sergei and my father, they are locked away in our house, discussing the future, plotting and scheming it all.

Yelena Rotcheva, the commander's wife, hosting my mother and me while the men talk business, serves us tea from her golden samovar. Her daughter, Olga, plays Mozart on the piano. Will I ever be such an elegant lady as Mrs. Rotcheva, with her Turkish carpets and fluent French? Or will she always be something unattainable, something glimpsed through the imported glass windows—the first of their kind in California—of her beautifully ornamented home?

In the end Sergei will keep some of the gold found in those mountains to the east, and it will be his duty to oversee the mines that will be dug there, on behalf of the tsar in faraway Saint Petersburg.

And we will be married before the start of the Great Lent, and by Easter I will know in my heart that something—someone—is growing inside me.

April 1842
The Gold Country—California Oblast

A knock at the door of our cabin jolts the baby awake and sets him crying while Evgenia, golden-haired and nearly three, seems nonplussed. I set down my sewing and go see who is there. A miner stands in my doorway, almost shaking with terror.

"What is it? Is something wrong at the mine?"

The man shakes his head. "No, nothing like that."

"Well, then, what is it?" And why was he coming to the wife of the head of operations? Unless he wanted Sergei, but Sergei was never home during the day. Sunup to sundown, he was working, making sure that the mines were running smoothly.

He takes a deep breath, preparing for what he is about to tell me. It must be bad. "Mexican troops, ma'am."

"Here?"

"Close. I saw them riding toward us, less than a day's ride away. They probably want the gold, madam."

I nod slowly. "Does my husband know?"

The miner shakes his head.

"All right, then. He needs to be told." I swallow my fear, deciding what to do. "I will tell him. You go to the mines, alert the other men."

He nods and leaves on his mission of warning.

I scoop up the baby and Evgenia follows without complaining. Thankfully, the office is not far, though the path is dusty. I find Sergei, oblivious to the threat that is, even as I take a moment to gaze upon my husband's last few moments of enviable ignorance, racing toward us. He is glancing over the accounting books, his face calm. For him, all is right with the world, and the gold keeps rolling in. When I first heard that there was gold in these hills, I never imagined that there would be such vast quantities—enough to send for more Alaskan and Russian men to mine the gold and build more settlements in these mountains that the Spanish called the Sierra Nevadas.

He looks up, and the color drains from his face. "What is it, Lara?"

The words come tumbling out of my mouth. "There are Mexican soldiers, coming here. For the gold. What should we do? The children? The gold? The mines . . ."

He steps away from the desk and holds me tightly. "Don't worry about the gold or the mines, my sunshine."

I nod. "But—the children. They can't stay here."

He shakes his head. "No. It isn't safe. I never should have—"

"And if you hadn't brought me here, we wouldn't have baby Misha, and I would be raising Zhenya all alone, at the colony." And that's when I realize exactly what I must do.

I embrace Sergei even tighter, knowing that I will not feel the safety of his arms again for quite some time. Knowing what the next several days hold for me and our children—a long ride back to the settlement, to my father. Torn, calloused hands and an exhausted horse will barely be enough to bring us to the safety of the stockade's redwood fence. And I will be forced to weather the coming war without my husband.

May 1843
Fortress Ross

We have survived the past year with very little word from Sergei. The war rages, with the tsar's troops on one side and the Mexican army on the other. The tsar seems determined to keep this land—land that, not too long ago, seemed useless. This outpost of a failing fur trade is thriving now—as a military encampment. What the Russian American Company failed to develop has become a boomtown with gold and war.

Today is different, finally. Today there are men on horseback screaming over the hills—those same hills that Sergei and Ivan tore across five years ago, shouting *"Zolota!"* and announcing the discovery of gold. And, once again, I find myself hoping, praying for word from Sergei. But now I am wondering—is he safe? Is he even still alive?

This time I can't go running up to the men—if I even have the nerve to, with what I might find out. Either way, I can't leave the men who need me, here in the old commandant's house, now converted into a hospital, with the elegant Yelena Rotcheva leading the colony's women in doing whatever we can to help the wounded men who are brought back to the fortress. There is very little I can do, except to offer comfort to the men, try to keep their wounds clean, and alert the only doctor if they worsen. Much of the time, my biggest service is holding their hands as they leave this world, praying with them at the moment of death. Most of the wounded do not survive, but I try to ensure that they do not die alone.

The chaos and horror provide a distraction from sitting at home, wondering if Sergei is alive or dead, if the fighting has reached the mines.

I look up from blotting a soldier's forehead with a cold cloth to peek out the window. The men are riding toward Commander Rotchev's house. Except for a few who are carrying the wounded.

I spot Ivan walking toward the hospital with a wounded man slung over his shoulders.

"I'll be right back, sir," I say to the solider as I leave, barely waiting for an affirmative moan before exiting.

Ivan is practically running across the grass toward me.

"Ivan, what is it?"

When he reaches the door of old Commander Rotchev's house, he sets the man down and I gasp at the sight. It's Oleg, Sergei's brother—the only blood relative who came with my husband to North America—unconscious and taking shallow, labored breaths. With Sergei away at the mines, the children and I are the only family Oleg has.

"He was shot in the leg, but . . ." Ivan stops explaining and rolls up the right leg of my brother-in-law's breeches. The wound is blackened, with red and purple borders, and the smell—I try to ignore the smell, but even after these months in the hospital I cannot completely erase the horror I feel now. Most men with wounds like this lose the leg, if they are lucky. If not, well, I don't want to think about that.

"Let's get him upstairs and I'll fetch the doctor for him." I take an arm and we manage his weight, though my shoulder wants to give out. If anything, Oleg is even taller and broader than Sergei, and I am tired from a long day's work.

There is an available bed in what used to be Rotchev's dining room and we muscle Oleg into it.

I find the doctor as he makes his rounds. "Please, Dr. Medvedev, I need you to see the man my brother brought in."

The doctor shakes his head. "Larissa Mikhailovna, you know perfectly well that they have brought many men here today—and with the battle raging near San Francisco, they will bring many more. Surely your brother's friend is not the only one deserving of my attention today."

"The man is Sergei's brother, Doctor. Please . . ." I feel tears well up in my eyes. "I know Oleg will probably die, but I refuse to do anything less than everything I can for Sergei's beloved brother. I will not face my husband, when this war is over, and tell him that I was too proud to beg a doctor to save Oleg's life."

To my relief, Dr. Medvedev nods and follows me into the old dining room, now crowded with beds and mats, since beds are in short supply.

Medvedev looks at the wound and shakes his head. "I can perhaps remove the leg, but . . ."

I nod slowly. "Do it. Sergei would want—"

Medvedev shakes his head. "I will try, of course, but it is unlikely he will live. He is unconscious already, which is a blessing, but . . . if the infection has spread, there is nothing I can do."

I pull myself up as straight as I can. "I will assist you, Doctor." Mainly because I cannot leave it to anyone else.

It is a long operation, but thankfully Oleg does not awaken during it. And yet—if so much pain cannot rouse him, what will?

And yet the next day his eyes blink open.

Oleg will live, albeit grieving the loss of his limb and his days as a soldier. In time he will learn that a war hero is perhaps even more attractive to the ladies. In a few short months the war will be over and Sergei will ride through the redwood gate, triumphant. The celebration will last for months. And Oleg will marry a part-Alaskan creole girl with startlingly blue eyes.

June 1855
New Saint Petersburg—California Oblast

Finally, the day has arrived and it is time for Sergei and me to host the first ball in the Governor's Mansion in New Saint Petersburg, the rechristened city formerly known as San Francisco. Years of rebuilding and new construction are behind us now. Despite that, the

Spanish foundations of the city are visible, beneath the surface of golden onion domes and baroque architecture. Unlike its namesake, New Saint Petersburg is cobbled together, the product of a clash of empires.

For more than ten years now, the city has been in Russian hands, but will it ever feel fully Russian?

That is the goal of evenings like this—to bring a bit of the Petersburg court to the New World. To put the war, and all of the death and destruction that it wrought, firmly behind us and establish our place here. This land is *nasha*—it is ours.

The servants have been overworked for weeks—shining samovars, dusting chandeliers, making hundreds of blini, opening tin upon tin of caviar. The wine will be flowing and the music will be playing and we will establish our city as worthy of its name.

And this is no dress rehearsal. Dignitaries from Saint Petersburg are here, and this is their welcome ball. With no chance to practice, this craftsman's daughter will have to impress visitors from the most elegant court in the world.

With a deep breath and one last glance in the mirror to ensure that my hair is perfect, I remind myself that I am no longer a craftsman's daughter or a miner's wife. No matter how much I might feel like an actress wearing a wealthy woman's dress and jewels, I know that my gems are not paste and the gold is real—much more real than my pedigree. No one who sees us tonight will see the poor man and the settler's daughter who didn't have enough money to marry. Instead, they will see a successful governor, the man who discovered gold in this land, the man who made this North American experiment an unqualified success. And they will see his wife, dripping with jewels, looking quite at home in the grandest house in California.

The tsar's treasury is full, and the tsar is thankful to those who made it possible. Most governors do not live this well, but no one begrudges us. New Saint Petersburg will be a showplace, the proof that Russia has arrived in North America, and we are not going anywhere.

No one will know the many hours of French lessons I endured to sound the part as well as look it. No one will know how I asked Yelena Rotcheva to teach me how to be a hostess, how many afternoons I spent with her before she and her husband left for Saint Petersburg, eager to return to their homeland after so many years on the frontier. Eager, really, to leave the running of the new California Oblast to Sergei. Now my wish is granted, and I am the elegant lady in the manor house, with Turkish carpets and golden samovars.

Later that evening, dancing with the trade minister, I know that I have made it—no one will doubt us now. The tsar's own minister, in my ballroom, dancing the waltz.

I glance over, and I see beautiful Zhenya, sixteen with golden hair in ringlets around her face and a dress from a Parisian pattern, dancing with the trade minister's son.

Before their visit is over, the young man will speak with Sergei, and their betrothal will be announced here in New Saint Petersburg, followed by a wedding in the capital. It will be my first visit to the capital of our empire. And my daughter will be the toast of Petersburg.

The Mighty and Me

Janis Thomas

I don't realize I'm a goner until it's too late. My mind refuses to process the information, refuses to allow for the possibility that my life is going to end on such a beautiful day. SoCal-cerulean sky, puffy white clouds, blazing sun, subtle breeze. This is a day meant for whimsy and laughter, skimboarding and paddle-surfing and s'mores. Not death. Especially not mine.

The tide that coaxed me in, coyly covering my toes with foam, now tugs at me harshly, pulling me farther from the safety of the shore.

For a moment I bob up and down impotently, staring at the specks the people on the beach have become. And I curse with rage at the Pacific, that mighty temptress, and at myself for my insouciance and my ego. I had to come in, I had to try, to feel, once again, the ocean's embrace after being apart for all those years. I pictured the reunion sweet. The Pacific was my first true friend. She took a chubby little girl and made her feel weightless and free. But now she is my enemy, an antagonist with all the power in the world. Why, I wonder, would she betray me? Because I'd been gone for so long, turned my back on her, moved away to the middle, where the only waves are of grain?

My arms strain, my hands plow through the choppy water as my feet kick uselessly beneath me. I want to wave at the lifeguard, but each time I lift my hand from the surface, I sink, falling prey to the voracious undertow. He wouldn't be watching for me anyway, even though he should be. Clearly. There are too many bikini-clad high school girls sashaying back and forth in front of him, stealing his attention away from the plump middle-aged mom lumbering to the surf. He likely doesn't even know I'm here. Well, I won't be for much longer.

A wave comes then, probably no more than a three- or four-foot face, but it might as well be a tsunami. I manage to suck in a quick breath before I am taken under. The force shoves me to the ocean floor, and my face scrapes against sand and broken bits of shell, but the wave is not through with me yet. It rolls me, over and over again, and I absently wonder whether I put the wash in the dryer before I left this morning, and who, oh, who, will do the laundry once I'm gone?

I thrash and flail, trying to gain purchase, but water is like wind, immaterial, intangible, impossible to grasp.

My lungs catch fire. *Air. Must have air.* My thoughts become muddled. Darkness, more complete than the deepest trench, is seeping into my brain. The animal, the primal, the id takes over.

I burst to the surface, coughing, choking, sputtering for air. I don't know how I did it, must have shoved off the bottom, but it doesn't matter because another wave is upon me. I am foolish. I shouldn't have come in. I am fifty-one, not fifteen. The ocean is no place for an overweight, middle-aged woman, no matter that she is strong and tough, tenacious and stubborn, and apparently—perilously—young at heart.

When my children were little, I would roll around with them on the floor. I slid down the waterslides behind them and glided down the snowy slopes right beside them, my butt perfectly encased in the rubber inner tube. I would ride the roller coasters and climb on the boogie board at the flow rider, even as the other mothers watched aghast. I didn't want to be the kind of parent that observes from the periphery of the action and becomes a ghost in her children's memories.

And if my children were ever embarrassed by the mother who jumped into the scrimmage with them and their friends, or bounced in the bounce house, or called "Marco" from the deep end of the pool, with eyes closed, awaiting their "Polos," they never let on, never humiliated me by asking me to excuse myself. Ruthie and Michael, my beautiful kids, who are at this moment standing in line at the snack bar to buy corn dogs and ice cream and have no idea that tomorrow they will be orphans.

I fooled myself with those pithy postulations, so frequent on Facebook: *You're only as old as you feel! Fifty is the new thirty! You're never too old to try new things! Embrace your inner child!* Like, like, like, like. Comment: Hallelujah, too right!

This wave is stronger than the last, and I hit the bottom so hard, all the precious air I was able to draw in rushes out of me. I feel the subluxation of several of my vertebrae and think of Dr. Ron. If I weren't about to die, I would find it amusing that one of my last thoughts as I pass into the hereafter is of my chiropractor.

She churns me again. Only this time, instead of fighting, I submit. Because my head is flooded with music and light and pictures from another time and another place. Another me, and yet still the same flesh and blood being hurled about and whose breath is being stolen away.

Oh, they built the ship Titanic to sail the ocean blue/And they thought they had a ship that the water would not leak through/Oh, the Lord's almighty hand said that ship would never land/It was sad when the great ship went down.

Girl Scout camp. I was eight. We sang that song, that spirited up-tempo happy tune that was in such stark contrast to the tragedy of which it spoke, but at eight years old, neither I nor any of my compatriots could conceive of tragedy or mortality or morbidity. So we sang it with gusto and danced with enthusiasm and laughed about how sad it was that the great ship went down.

My troop won the human pyramid competition. I was the anchor, the body that is on the bottom and in the middle. All the weight of the girls above rests on the anchor. I held fast, held strong, even as my arms shook and my muscles screamed, as sweat poured down my face and dripped onto the dirt beneath me. I did not fold. That was who I was. That was who I was when I was eight.

That is who I am now.

I break free of my liquid confines, erupting from below like a buoy too long held under. I suck in great gasps of air—the universe might collapse from all the air I swallow. The sun, high in the sky, sears my retinas, blinding me, but that's okay. That's fine. I am breathing.

I see it before it hits me, another wave. The Pacific is ruthless in her constancy. I inhale all the way to my belly and dive below just as the crest of the wave falls. Beneath, beyond the tumultuous aftermath of the crash, the sea is calm. And for a moment I am eight again, twisting, turning, stroking, somersaulting, gliding through the water, playing with my oldest friend.

I am farther out now. The land, the beach, appear as a mirage might, shimmering on the horizon, a goal that may or may not be reached. A promise that might or might not be kept.

I was the anchor in that pyramid. Not the kind of anchor that plummets to the bottom. The kind that holds fast, holds strong.

I was a mother who jumped on trampolines and played laser tag and rode zip lines. Who taught her children to take chances, to be brave, to be fierce, to live and love and laugh. And jump in the ocean whenever possible.

I push toward shore. A wave takes me. I time it and roll, then stroke, kick, stroke, kick. The Pacific fights me. Perhaps she doesn't want to let me go. Perhaps she has been lonely without me. I crawl forward only to have her drag me back. I don't give in, but the cost is great. Every muscle from the base of my skull to the tips of my toes seizes. Pain and adrenaline square dance within me.

I tread water for a few precious seconds to get my bearings. The specks on the beach are now people again, frolicking, flirting, bronzing their skin. Atop his tower, the lifeguard has taken notice of me through his binoculars.

He'll come for me, I think. *He'll come for me if I need him to.*

I take a breath and thrust ahead. I feel the rise of the water behind me, a sneak attack launched by a treacherous foe bent on denying me the shore. But it's my own fault because I could have seen it, could have prepared myself if only I'd looked back before moving forward.

It swallows me.

I think of Peter. He'll say what he always says. "What was she thinking?" The question most often revisited during our beleaguered marriage asked by the peripheral parent who watched from the sidelines. "What were you thinking?"

I was thinking, Peter, that I might be growing old, but I don't want to grow up. I was thinking that I don't want to die before I'm dead.

With hands and feet, I push away from the ocean floor. The salt water stings the countless abrasions all over my body. My left calf pops and spasms. My shoulders ache. My head pounds. I gird myself with all the strength I know I possess, the strength of the pyramid anchor, and I go. And I go. The waves come, and still I go until, finally, I feel the sand and shells beneath my feet.

I stagger from the surf. My arms feel like socks full of cement. My legs are leaden and I am unable to lift my feet, so I create parallel troughs all the way to the soft, dry sand. A little girl building a sandcastle with a red Solo cup squeals with delight.

"You made moats for my castle!"

My lungs haven't recovered. I can only offer the girl a smile.

I bend at the waist, rest my hands on my knees, and slowly breathe in and breathe out. I still can't comprehend that I made it. Or how I made it. My knees buckle, but I don't let myself fall. I made it this far. I won't collapse now.

A shadow appears on the sand beside me. The lifeguard. I can tell by the shape of his straw hat. I glance up at him. He isn't looking at me. He's looking out at her, at the mighty Pacific. I stand up straight and follow his gaze.

"You okay?" he asks quietly.

"I am," I tell him. A slight fib that will become the truth very soon.

He nods. "I'm pretty impressed that you made it. Not many people could have, you know."

He walks away, calls out irreverently to a nubile young woman with sun-bleached tresses who laughs coyly in response.

As my heartbeat returns to normal, I continue to gaze at the Pacific. She used to be my friend. I no longer know who she is to me.

But I know who I am to myself.

"Mom, want a corn dog?" comes the beloved voice from behind me. "We got three."

Contributors

D. P. Lyle is the Macavity and Benjamin Franklin Silver Award winning and Edgar (2), Agatha, Anthony, Scribe, Shamus, Silver Falchion, and USA Today Best Book (2) Award nominated author of seventeen books, both fiction and nonfiction. He has worked as a story consultant for many novelists and with the writers of the television shows *Law & Order, CSI: Miami, Diagnosis Murder, Monk, Judging Amy, Cold Case, House, Medium, Women's Murder Club, The Glades*, and *Pretty Little Liars*.

Biff (Harold D.) Baker is based in Irvine, California, and has worked for twenty years in the educational software industry. With a doctorate in Russian and comparative literature from Brown University, he was previously on the faculty of the University of California, Irvine, has published on a variety of topics, and is currently completing the thriller novel *Red Snow, Gold Clouds* together with his wife, Marianna, and daughter, Anna.

Phyllis Blake is a pianist by training and writes fiction that often centers around music performance. Born in Arizona, she grew up in La Jolla and has lived and worked in Orange County, California, most of her adult life.

PJ Colando writes comedy and satire with a literary bent. Her published work includes short stories, personal essays, and three books, two fiction and one nonfiction. Follow her boomer humor blog on pjcolandoblog.com.

Rose de Guzman writes young adult and alternate history but never alternate history for young adults. She lives in Southern Orange County, California, where her short story "Melting the Ice" was featured in the Romance Writers of America anthology *Romancing the Pages* and where she is a municipal liaison for National Novel Writing Month.

Lani Forbes is a middle school teacher from Huntington Beach, California. She writes young adult science fiction and fantasy.

Wanda Green is a fiction and nonfiction writer. She has written and directed several gospel skits and plays produced in churches on the East Coast.

Dana Hammer is the author of two novels, *The Taxidermist* and *Rosemary's Baby Daddy*. She loves Disneyland.

Catheryn Hull is an artist and a writer living in Orange County, California. She has published many how-to books on entertaining and self-improvement and started writing fiction ten years ago.

Steven G. Jackson (stevengjackson.com) is the author of the highly rated thriller novel *The Zeus Payload*, as well as five produced stage plays.

Maddie Margarita writes stories of suspense, humor, and fantasy. She is the recipient of a Southern California Writers' Conference award for fiction and produces LitUp! OC, a smart, amped-up literary salon in Orange County, California.

Jeffrey J. Michaels crafts tales that range from mystical fantasies set in the mists of history to emotionally enchanting short stories contemplating life and love in contemporary California. He offers inspiring workshops, including The Long and Short of Storytelling and Write from the Heart.

Anne Moose is a working writer and the author of *Arkansas Summer*, a novel about love and racial terror in the Jim Crow South. She lives with her husband, Peter Dingus, in Mission Viejo, California.

Andrew R. Nixon is an author currently living in Las Vegas, Nevada. His books include *50 Shades of Grades: My Journey through Wacademia* and *Three Lives of Peter Novak*. His newspaper columns have appeared in the *Las Vegas Sun*.

Jo Perry is the author of three dark, comic mysteries, *Dead Is Better*, *Dead Is Best*, and *Dead Is Good* from Fahrenheit Press. She lives in Los Angeles, California.

D. J. Phinney is a Southern California native, published technical author, former Air Force captain, and practicing civil engineer. He divides his time between Irvine and Pasadena, California. His debut historical novel, *The Anaheim Beauties Valencia Queen*, is scheduled for publication in early 2018.

Jo Ellen Pitzer enjoys writing young adult fantasy. She lives and works in Orange County, California.

Casey Pope writes novels in the mainstream/upmarket category (literary/commercial hybrid) and in a variety/mashup of genres. His debut novel, *A Love Life like Karmic Disaster*, is a contemporary "love story" inspired by Mary Shelley's novel *Frankenstein*. Visit www .FugitiveJusticeMedia.com.

David Putnam has done it all during his career in law enforcement: he worked in narcotics, violent crimes, criminal intelligence, hostage rescue, SWAT, and internal affairs, to name just a few areas. He is the recipient of many awards and commendations for heroism. *The Vanquished*, the fourth book in his Bruno Johnson series, followed the best-selling and critically acclaimed *The Disposables*, *The Replacements*, and *The Squandered*. His fifth Bruno Johnson thriller will be released in 2018. Visit DavidPutnamBooks.com.

Glenda Brown Rynn writes short stories (one of which was nominated for a Pushcart Prize), essays, and articles. Her monthly write-ups of the guest speakers at the Southern California Writers Association are in its online newsletter at ocwriter.com.

Janis Thomas is a critically acclaimed women's fiction author and popular writing coach. She lives in Huntington Beach, California, with her terrific hubby, amazing offspring, and crazy canines.

Julie Wells is a marriage and family therapist who loves to help people restore loving relationships. Her great loves in life are her seven siblings, two children, and one amazing husband of thirty-three years.

Acknowledgments

The Southern California Writers Association would like to thank the following patrons for their gracious support of our vision:

PJ Colando
Hasen and Nancy Djavarian
Joe Ide
Doug Lyle
Sharmyn McGraw
Francine Tarlov Porricelli
Marty Roth
Anne Sallier, Book Carnival
Joanne Porricelli Scofield
Ed and Analee Speer
Colonel and Mrs. John Tighe
Mary Lou Tighe
Ken and Cindy Williams

These patrons are champions of writers everywhere, especially those in the SCWA community, and join us in promoting the welfare, fellowship, spirit, and continuing education of writers at all stages of their writing journey.

Thank you also to our members, whose participation and support enable SCWA to grow and thrive, and to the SCWA Board—Larry Porricelli, Steve Jackson, Don Westenhaver, and Maddie Margarita—who along with our Editorial Board—Steve Jackson, Sharon Goldinger, and Pam Sheppard—nurtured this anthology from an exciting idea to publication.

Last but not least, SCWA extends our heartfelt gratitude to our editor, D. P. Lyle, whose talent and inspiration enabled us to fulfill this dream.

Thank you for your unending support.